Country Roads,
PAINTED SKIES

HEART-TUGGING STORIES OF LIFE,
CHOICE, AND GROWING UP

JUDIE GULLEY

Pacific Press® Publishing Association

Nampa, Idaho

Oshawa, Ontario, Canada

www.pacificpress.com

Designed by Dennis Ferree
Photo by Tim Bieber Getty Images

Additional copies of this book are available by calling toll free
1-800-765-6955 or by visiting www.AdventistBookCenter.com

Library of Congress Cataloging-in-Publication Data

Gulley, Judie.
Country roads, painted skies : hart-tugging stories of life, choice,
and growing up / Judie Gulley.
p. cm.
ISBN: 0-8163-2058-6 (pbk.)
1. Schools. 2. Students. 3. Bus drivers. 4. Country life.
5. Maturation (Psychology). I. Title.

PS3557.U4486C68 2005
813'.54—dc22   2004057336

05 06 07 08 09 · 5 4 3 2 1

DEDICATION

This book is dedicated to
my awesome grandson, Jeremy, the most wonderful grandson a grandma could ever ask for;
my beautiful granddaughter, Madison, the most wonderful
granddaughter a grandma could ever ask for;
and my great friends, Barb Foster and Chris Walkowicz,
who have read every story in this book. Thanks, you guys,
for all the help, encouragement, and prayers!

CONTENTS

Sons and Daughters, Moms and Dads

1. The First Day · · · · · 9

2. A Mother and Daughter · · · · · 12

3. Walk a Mile · · · · · 15

4. Playing God · · · · · 19

5. Mistaken Expectations · · · · · 22

6. Daddy's Little Girl · · · · · 25

7. A Father and Son · · · · · 28

8. The Best Dad · · · · · 31

Prayers and Promises

1. Life Lesson · · · · · 36

2. Eyes of a Stranger · · · · · 40

3. Never Stop, Mike · · · · · 44

4. Time to Heal · · · · · 48

5. Sticks and Stones · · · · · 51

6. The List · · · · · 54

7. A Moment in Time · · · · · 58

8. Understanding · · · · · 61

Christmas Wishes

1. The Least Ones · · · · · 66

2. A Little Help to Find the Way · · · · · 70

3. Friendship Is Everything · · · · · 74

4. The Best Gift · · · · · 77

5. A Love Story · · · · · 80

Country Roads

1. When It Counts · · · · · 86

2. Playing With Fire · · · · · 89

3. What Will Be · · · · · 94

4. Paybacks · · · · · 97

5. Risk Taker · · · · · 99

6. A Wasted Life · · · · · 102

7. Remember · · · · · 106

8. Forgiving · · · · · 109

Fears, Tears, and Summer Dreams

1. Every Thorn Has a Rose · · · · · 114

2. Dragon Slayer · · · · · 119

3. Underneath It All · · · · · 123

4. Not Like Me · · · · · 126

5. Kindergarten Starfish · · · · · 130

6. Baskets of Bluebells · · · · · 134

7. Someone Cares · · · · · 137

8. Just Another Summer · · · · · 141

Section 1

Sons and Daughters, Moms and Dads

THE FIRST DAY

The morning is steamy and still. The sun, just clearing the horizon, promises an August day brilliant with heat and humidity. In the southwest, I can see clouds gathering, threatening a late-summer storm.

Typical of the first day of school.

I guide my washed and polished school bus down the narrow country road between fields of dry, nearly-ready-to-harvest corn, squinting to see through the glass reflecting the first light. The summer is over. I'm anxious to see the changes in the kids I left behind in the spring, interested to meet the newcomers who will replace last year's graduates. A never-ending cycle for a school bus driver. Not always a happy one. I miss many of the kids who have passed through my life. I wonder what their lives have become and whether they sometimes remember the bus driver and the hours we spent together.

Doubtful, I reluctantly concede to myself. From year to year, I watch them grow from wide-eyed preschoolers to awesome, almost-adult seniors; from their first steps onto the bus to their first steps into the world. Their lives are filled with so many wonders, so many other exciting "firsts," it's not likely they ever think back to a hot, dusty, tedious bus ride to school.

I see a little boy and his mom standing by the mailbox ahead and, with a smile, I switch on the overhead flashers and step on the brake. Jeremy Allan will be my first stop this year. This is his very first day of kindergarten. He stares up at the red and yellow flashers, his huge blue eyes wide with awe, and moves closer to his mother, who rests a protective hand on his blond head. The brand-new backpack strapped to his back is decorated with the most popular television cartoon characters. His clothes are neat and new, too; his hair freshly cut and slicked into the latest little boys' style.

The bus stops in a swirl of dust and mist reflecting the early morning sun, and I open the door.

And take a good look at the future of the world.

Jeremy looks at the bus, at me, and then up to his mother for reassurance. She smiles and rubs her hand over his hair. She glances up at me and with her eyes begs me to please watch over this small wonder she loves with all her heart.

She and I both know and understand that with this bus ride, Jeremy is setting off on his journey through life. His world will be forever changed. Small-boy steps will grow to lanky strides and lead him to wonderful places, both mythical and real. He'll join a world of computerized technology and pyramids, the Internet and dinosaurs, traveling stormy seas and painted skies and places where swirling sands blow ancient boats down the Nile. He'll learn a lesson that adults often forget—that life is an ongoing process, a journey that begins with mothers and fathers and travels country roads into classrooms and beyond.

As it should be. But so difficult for those left behind. Those letting go. Other worlds will be changed forever, too.

I smile at Jeremy's mother, and she accepts my reassurance. She bends to hug her little wanderer. He hugs back quickly, pushes away, and climbs up into the bus, a big boy now. I see his mother's hand reach out as though to gather him back. Then she lets it fall helplessly to her side. The first step has been taken. In the distance, in the gathering cloud mass, I see lightning strike the ground.

I shut the door, the red flashers stop, and the summer comes to an end.

No earth-shattering events this morning. Jeremy is just one of thousands of children who laced up his tennis shoes and strapped on his backpack to begin his journey. The tenuous link between a mother and son has been stretched just a bit more.

The First Day

No, I think, as I steer the bus down the road, dust swirling under the wheels to mix with the morning mist, *Jeremy probably won't remember this hot, humid August day with the hint of fall in the air. But his mother will. She may not recall the rustle of the morning breeze through dry corn in the field across the road or the noisy chirps of the crickets and buzzing cicadas, but she'll remember forever that a yellow school bus gathered up a small blond boy and traveled into the future, away from the gathering storm.*

A MOTHER AND DAUGHTER

As her school-bus driver, I'd suspected for a long time that life was not easy for fourteen-year-old Lori Jackson. But it wasn't until a quiet, warm, early fall day that I found out how bad it really was.

She wasn't waiting when I pulled up to her driveway. I braked to a stop, honked the horn, and waited. Nothing. I had the bus in gear, ready to go on, when I saw the house door slam open. Lori shot out, running toward us as best she could with an armload of books and a gym bag slung over one shoulder. Her heavy blond hair, still damp from her morning shower, swung wildly about her shoulders. There were pretty pink patches on her cheeks when she reached the bus.

"Sorry," she said as she struggled up the steps, giving me a small smile.

"Lori Ann!" The woman's voice was loud and slurred.

Lori froze, then turned. I saw the woman staggering across the unkempt lawn, holding a pair of gym shoes. She was dressed in a long stained robe that billowed open with every gust of wind. Her hair hung in tangled wisps about her face.

"Hey, a crazy woman!" someone in the back hooted.

The pink on Lori's cheeks deepened to bright red. "Shut up!" she hissed between clenched teeth, not bothering to see who had said it. She dropped her books in the aisle and caught the woman at the bus door, pulling the robe shut and tying it securely.

"Mom," she whispered, "you shouldn't be out here."

A Mother and Daughter

Mrs. Jackson fell against the side of the bus, and Lori put an arm around her waist to support her.

"But you leff your . . . your . . ." Lori's mother couldn't seem to find the word she wanted and instead just held out the shoes, her hand shaking.

Even from where I sat, I could smell the cheap whiskey.

Lori looked up at me.

"Just go on," she whispered.

I hesitated. This situation had all the signs of being something I needed to keep my nose out of, but I hated to leave her there. I made a decision.

"I'll be back to get you in my car," I whispered back. "Just as soon as I run the bus route."

As I pulled away, I looked in the overhead mirror and watched Lori helping her mother toward the house. The older woman leaned on her daughter.

The noise and laughter on the bus had quieted down to a strange, embarrassed silence. I was glad. My mind was whirling, and I didn't have the emotional reserves to deal with a bunch of unanswerable questions and remarks.

Forty-five minutes later, after I'd dropped off the last of the school kids and returned the bus to the bus garage, I was back in Lori's driveway. This time her steps down the driveway were slower. She slid into the front seat of my car, taking great care not to look at me.

"Is your mom all right?" I asked.

Lori nodded. I saw a small smile touch her lips. "Yeah, she's fine. She had another drink and went back to bed. She'll be there until I come home." The blond teenager closed her eyes and leaned her head against the back of the seat.

"How about you?" I said. "Are you going to be OK?"

She glanced at me then. "Sure. I've gotten used to this over the years. At first when Dad left, I was too little to take care of her very good. Now she pretty much does what I tell her to do."

It took my breath away to think of this child taking on responsibility for an alcoholic parent. Right now her biggest worry should have been what clothes to wear to school or whether or not her favorite boy was going to ask her for a date.

"Don't you have any family—aunts or uncles—anybody who will help?"

Lori turned toward me. Her eyes were flat and filled with a pain so adult that it made me ache.

"Alcoholics pretty much screw up everything they touch," she said. "And believe me, she's 'touched' every friend and relative we ever had. She's even called the parents of my school friends, asking for 'just two dollars for gas money.' That's why most of the kids don't hang around me now."

My fingers were welded to the steering wheel as we pulled into the high-school parking lot and stopped. I wanted to get my hands on Mrs. Jackson and shake her until she saw what she was doing to her daughter.

"If there's any good at all to be found in this," I told Lori, "it's that the whole thing has made you a strong person. You won't make the same mistakes your mother has made."

Lori didn't answer. She looked down at her books for a moment, her hair falling about her face like a soft, golden curtain.

"We all make our own mistakes," she said.

She opened the door and started to slide out. Impulsively, I reached over to give her a hug.

And then I learned a lesson about life, and mothers and daughters, and the way things are in the world.

I smelled liquor on Lori's breath.

I drew away, not knowing what to do or say. Or think. She stared at me steadily. There was no apology in her eyes, no remorse. Just a deep and bitter sorrow that came clear from her soul.

"It helps me get through the day," she whispered. Then she gathered her books together and walked away.

WALK A MILE

When the bus rocked curiously as I headed out into the country on my Friday afternoon route, it took only one glance to confirm my suspicions. Ricky Luedke and Shawn Minor were locked in mortal combat again in the last seats. If it had been my choice, it could have continued. I didn't care if it was a fight to the death, but . . . well . . . they were only kids. Not to mention I'd probably lose my job if they killed each other!

So I sighed, pulled to the side of the road, and sauntered to the back, trying to appear concerned.

"Hey, guys," I yelled. "Break it up! Now!"

They continued to roll around in the aisle. The little kids in front were hanging over the seats, pulling their legs out of the way, starting to choose sides.

"Be quiet," I ordered. I finally grabbed a shirt collar and felt it give as I pulled. *Now I'll probably get in trouble for ripping the kid's shirt,* I thought. *Bummer!*

The one I pulled away was Shawn Minor, his heavy dark hair hanging over his pale blue eyes like a sheepdog. He was panting furiously, struggling to get to Ricky Luedke. Not struggling as hard as I knew he could, though.

I pushed him into a seat and put my other hand on Ricky's bony chest. "Sit!" I snarled. He sat, his shoulder length blond hair swinging wildly. Both of them tried to catch their breath, staring daggers across the aisle.

"This is it," I fumed. "I've told you for the last time. Now I'm asking Mr. Anderson for in-school suspensions for the both of you."

Rick and Shawn weren't bad kids . . . just annoying. And I'd been annoyed enough.

But when I wrote the suspension slips out and turned them in to Principal Anderson that afternoon, I just didn't have a clue.

"Your presence is requested in the superintendent's office," Mac told me the next Monday day. "Wear a helmet." He smiled. I was afraid to ask.

When I walked into Mr. Anderson's office, a small, trim woman, dressed in a tan jacket and pants I could describe only as elegant, rose to her feet from the chair beside the desk. Her dark hair framed her creamy face perfectly. Her pale blue eyes were made of steel.

Mr. Anderson opened his mouth to introduce us, but he never got the chance. I knew who she had to be, anyway. Her eyes were flashing the same daggers I'd seen in Shawn's the day before.

"I will not stand for this," the woman said, each word chiseled from ice. "This boy . . . Ricky someone? . . . keeps pushing Shawn around, getting him into trouble. I've had enough. I want the punishment to be given where it's deserved."

"Mrs. Minor," I began, "the boys were equally . . ."

I stopped as the door behind Mrs. Minor opened. The woman who came in could have been Ricky's grandmother. Red-rimmed eyes set in dark, weary sockets, clothes rumpled, glasses askew, Mrs. Luedke looked, at best, weary and in need of sleep. She shut the door, checked her watch, glanced around the room.

"Hi," she said brightly, trying a smile. "I have to be back to work in twenty minutes. Could someone tell me what's going on, please?"

"Of course," Mrs. Minor explained as if to a small child. "Apparently, your son . . . Richard? . . . has been causing trouble for my Shawn on the bus."

I could see the hair on the back of Mrs. Luedke's neck stand up. Mr. Anderson moved behind his desk, and I wished I could have gone with him.

Walk a Mile

"Oh?" Ricky's mom said softly. "And how is that?"

"Richard has been picking on my son, starting fights on the bus. Shawn has been raised a little . . . differently. He knows we don't allow rowdiness on the bus or in school."

Mrs. Luedke's voice was even softer. "Are you implying Ricky hasn't been raised correctly?"

Mrs. Minor sensed things weren't going well. A red flush spread from her neck to her cheeks.

"Some of us stay home and take care of our children," she snapped. "Some of us care."

I was hunting for the bomb shelter. At the very least, I expected Ricky's mom to grab Mrs. Minor by the throat. Her reaction shocked us all. She sat down.

"Because I go to a job every day, you think I don't care about my kids?" she said. "Do you think anything you can say can make me feel any more guilty about not being there for them?" She took a deep breath. "I wish I had the choices you have. Unfortunately, my kids have to eat, and they have to have a roof over their heads, and I'm the only one who can do that. Before you judge me as uncaring, try 'walking a mile in my shoes,' as the saying goes." She laughed, and there was no humor in the sound. "You don't even have to do a mile. From here to the door will work just fine. You can get your self-righteous attitude out of my face. I worked fifteen hours last night for minimum wage, and I don't need to be judged by someone whose major decision this morning was what color shoes to wear."

The room was silent. Mrs. Minor was carved in stone. Then, we were all stunned to see her rise to her feet. "Excuse me," she said. With crisp, measured strides, she walked to the door, opened it, and left. The door clicked shut behind her.

I turned to Mr. Anderson. His mouth was hanging open just like mine, but neither of us had any words. Then I heard the door click open.

"Good afternoon," Mrs. Minor said, as though she'd never been in the room before. She walked right to Mrs. Luedke and extended one gloved hand. "It's nice to meet you. I'm Shawn's mother," she said softly, as though they hadn't been talking just a moment before.

"I hear our sons are in a bit of a pickle, but I'm sure we can work it out."

An apology. Her smile was both stiff and shaky.

Without missing a beat, Ricky's mom got to her feet, shook the offered hand, and said, "I'm sure we can."

Forgiveness. She smiled too.

I watched them talk, knowing everything would be fine with Ricky and Shawn. These moms were both class acts. Now that they'd established the ground rules, they could work on the problem together.

PLAYING GOD

Fall is always a learning experience for a school-bus driver. Long-time riders have graduated or moved away; new kids start as kindergarteners or move into the district. It's interesting to meet the new ones, look into their eyes, see their reactions to my smile and "Good morning." The response isn't always what I'd expect or even wish for.

That's why I was so surprised that September morning when Mark Andrews's mom was waiting for me at the end of the driveway.

Andrews, a short, square-faced eighth-grader was a new rider on my bus, but I'd already resorted to planning terrible things in my mind—taping his mouth shut, tying his wrists to his ankles, perhaps merely strapping him to the top of the bus.

Not that he was a bad kid. Mouthy, irritating, and obnoxious maybe, perhaps even off-color, but not really bad.

I would have preferred bad. Then I could have kicked him off the bus. But how do you harshly discipline a child who, after listening to three minutes of tirade from a furious bus driver, can look up with eyes as big and round and blue as a robin's egg and say, "Are you fixing your hair differently? It looks great!"

He never failed to stop me speechless in mid-sentence. So, somehow I would continue to tolerate his chatter, the way he teased the girls and made them shriek, even his mad dashes to the bus after I had waited and waited and just started to pull away from his driveway.

The afternoon his mother stopped me I wondered if she was talk-ing about the same Mark I had been hauling to school everyday.

"Mark has told me you've been very kind to him," she said. Her smile was apologetic. "I know he can be a bother." Her eyes, the same startling blue as Mark's, avoided meeting mine. "I don't know how to ask you this." A small woman, she also had the same square jaw, which gave her a belligerent, defensive look. Only the eyes, tired and hopeless, betrayed her.

"We don't know anyone here," her voice trailed off.

I knew Mark had signed up for the free lunch program and that the area food pantry made a weekly trip to the Andrews's home. I had never seen any kind of vehicle in their driveway, so I assumed Mrs. Andrews wasn't working. Did she intend to ask for money?

"Tricia? My little girl?" She made the statement a question. "She needs to go to the doctor's office twice a week for the next six weeks. I don't have any way to take her."

The conversation was taking a turn I didn't like. My life was busy, and I sure didn't want to be responsible for taking a strange child into town.

I glanced nervously back at the couple of kids left on the bus.

"Have you tried the school?" I asked. "Maybe they'd help."

She shook her head, her gray-streaked hair falling softly about her face. "I called there and also the Child and Family Services in town," she said. Her voice was almost a whisper. "I thought maybe . . ." she hesitated, then took a deep breath and smiled. "Well, if you can think of anyone who might take us, could you let me know? I'd be much obliged."

It was my turn to smile at the antiquated cliché she used, the rural drawl spilling over her tongue.

"I sure will," I said, feeling guilt settling into my chest like a stone as she turned to walk away. Anger rose up to dance around my guilt. Why should I have to be the one to help this woman? Why did I have to give my time to take a strange child to the doctor? And most important of all, why did I feel guilty?

"Mrs. Andrews?" I called out as she walked away. She turned, her eyebrows raised into question marks.

"I'll be glad to take her," I said—hating her, hating myself for being weak, and hating the little girl called Tricia for infringing upon my life.

Monday morning after my bus run was completed, I pulled my car into the Andrews's driveway and tapped the horn. Mark's mom appeared at once in the doorway and rushed down the broken path. I had the uneasy feeling she was terrified of making me wait.

"Mornin'," she said breathlessly. "This here's Tricia." She slid into the seat beside me. Peering from her arms was a tiny blond child with eyes so big and blue it was easy for a heart to get lost in them. But I steeled my resolve. I wasn't about to let these people take advantage of me.

"Mrs. Andrews," I said firmly, as I backed out of the driveway. "I really have a lot of things to do. I'll be glad to take Tricia a day or two, but I'd sure appreciate it if you could find someone else after that."

She nodded, not looking up. As I turned out into the highway, I thought I saw a tear escape down her cheek.

The hate turned inward. *How dare she!* I thought. *How dare she make me feel so guilty!* My knuckles turned white on the steering wheel.

The little girl continued to stare at me until I could no longer resist the temptation to look back.

"Are you God?" she asked aloud.

I was shocked into a smile. "I don't think so," I answered. "Why would you ask such a thing?"

"Because," she said, "Mommy and Mark have been praying to God for a way to take me to the doctor. I thought maybe you were God."

I gripped the steering wheel tightly to keep the car on the road until I could breathe again.

Mrs. Andrews hugged her daughter close. "She's only three," she said apologetically. "She doesn't know."

She knows the important stuff, I thought. The aggravation and impatience washed from my heart like a warm shower of summer rain. *I'm so sorry,* I prayed silently. *Forgive me.*

"I'm sure not God," I teased Tricia. "But I am a pretty good driver. I guess if Mark doesn't drive me crazy, I can drive you to the doctor."

She laughed as we drove down the road.

MISTAKEN EXPECTATIONS

Cindy Olson was just two weeks from graduating. She was vale-dictorian of our small-town high school, and several good colleges had already offered terrific scholarships. I knew she was nervous and excited. But the look on her face that fall morning as she climbed the steps into the bus was one of fear.

I smiled at her, but she didn't even look up. She almost ran past me to the back and threw herself into a seat next to her best friend, Marcia Williams. I watched in the overhead mirror as she sat close to Marcia and whispered into her ear. Marcia's eyes grew big and round, and she frowned.

My heart quickened as I put the bus in gear. Cindy was one of my favorites. I'd taken her to school since her kindergarten days and enjoyed her more every year. A cheerful, confident girl, she was well liked by teachers and classmates alike.

There was no way of knowing what kind of problem she was con-fiding to Marcia, but I knew her well enough to realize she wouldn't be this upset over anything that was unimportant.

At the high school, I had my first clue.

"Well, I'd be embarrassed, too," Marcia muttered under her breath. "A baby, for Pete's sake! What did your folks say?"

It took my breath away, and Cindy's answer scared me even more.

"I can't talk to them about it," she said, shaking her head as they walked away from the bus. "They wouldn't understand."

Mistaken Expectations

I couldn't think of anything else all day. Sweet little Cindy expecting a baby? She'd had such hopes . . . such dreams for her future. Even worse, she was afraid to confide in her parents. Now she was alone and terrified.

When Cindy got on the bus that afternoon, I stopped her. "Cindy, listen," I began uncertainly. "I don't want to come across as a busybody, but . . ." I hesitated and took a deep breath.

She waited, a puzzled expression on her face.

"I know about the baby." I blurted it out in a whisper.

Her eyes widened with surprise.

"I overheard you this morning," I explained. "I'm sorry for eavesdropping, but listen, you've got to talk to your mom and dad. Everything will be so much better if you'll just confide in them."

"Do you really think so?" Cindy looked at me doubtfully.

"Of course!" I rushed on, encouraged that she was listening to me. "You've got to give them a chance."

Cindy was silent. Did the look in her eyes soften just a little? I hoped so. After a minute, without a word, she turned and went back to her seat.

I hoped against hope that maybe my pitiful little speech would help her make up her mind.

I was so distracted that when the phone rang that night, I had trouble understanding who was calling.

"This is Carl Olson," the man said. I frowned, trying to remember where I'd met someone called *Carl Olson*.

"Cindy's dad," he added.

"Oh . . . yes," I said weakly, reaching for a chair. "Can I help you?"

"I just want to thank you," he said. "Cindy said that you spoke with her on the bus today—told her she should talk to us. I just wanted you to know that she did, and we got everything straightened out. We really want to thank you."

"I'm so glad," I breathed, a feeling of relief pouring over me like a bucket of warm water.

"We're really excited about the baby," he continued. "We've waited and prayed for such a long time. Sixteen years. We just thought it'd never happen. You can't imagine how thrilled we are."

What? I sat straighter, my ears quivering indignantly. What kind of parents were these? What was going on here?

"Most parents aren't quite this understanding," I said faintly.

"Oh, I know at first Cindy was upset. You know how teenagers are. But now that we've talked it over, I think she's as excited as we are. A new baby in the house! Can you imagine?"

"I'm glad that you're so happy." I was unable to keep the coldness out of my voice. He didn't seem to notice.

"We thank you so much for your kindness. Marge would have called herself, but she's had morning sickness so bad . . ."

Something started ticking in a small corner of my brain.

"Marge?" I repeated stupidly.

"My wife. Ever since we found out that she's expecting, she's been sick. She'll probably feel a lot better now. I think a lot of it had to do with how Cindy took the news. You know kids. They always think of their parents as ancient—too old for this sort of thing. She was a little stunned and embarrassed."

"Yes," I replied brilliantly, too stunned and embarrassed myself to say any more. I did manage to say goodbye right on cue, although I had no idea of what he'd said before that.

After a while, when I could breathe again, I realized what a truly marvelous day it had been. The Olsons were expecting after sixteen years of prayers. Cindy wasn't going to have to give up her college plans.

And best of all, if I kept my mouth shut, no one would ever know what a dunce I'd almost made of myself!

DADDY'S LITTLE GIRL

The second full week of school, a very special program was given to the elementary grades in our small town. Afterwards, school officials called all staff personnel together to tell us what to watch for.

"Teachers and bus drivers hear things the kids wouldn't tell anyone else," Principal Anderson said. "And there are certain outward signs . . ."

As he spoke, we all glanced at each other self-consciously. *Not any of my kids*, I thought.

I knew them all . . . and their families. In many cases, the parents themselves were former passengers on my bus. For the most part, my kids seemed happy and well-adjusted, none were sending out any of the subtle signals Mr. Anderson was asking us to watch for. "They're told the adult is sick and needs help," he said. "Sometimes it makes them more willing to come forward, when they think they can help Dad or Grandpa or . . ."

I swallowed painfully. No, I was positive there were no hints of anything so inconceivably horrible as sexual abuse going on within any of the families on my route.

Except that sometimes I wondered about . . .

I shook my head and tried to sweep away the nagging thought as it drifted past like smoke. *Just my imagination in high gear*, I told myself. *A case of casual neglect, at worst. Nothing more.*

But the next day or so, eight-year-old Linda Wilson's face began to flash in my mind like an out-of-control neon sign. Such a thin, scraggly haired little thing. My heart had gone out to her two years ago when she first climbed up the bus steps as a kindergartner. Linda always had an unwashed look, her clothes often rumpled and stained as though they'd just been pulled out of a throw-away box. Her breakfast was usually a handful of candy she hastily gulped as she ran to the bus. One morning she met me with a frightened look and a bloody nose. I told the school nurse about it and found myself caught up in a flurry of outraged activity from the school and the local Child and Family Welfare department. Linda looked a little better after that— neater and better fed.

I was glad when Cassandra Larson became her friend. Both Cassie's mom and dad had ridden my bus most of their school years and married not long after graduation. They'd been the kind of kids who were a joy to take to school—happy and friendly and popular with the others. And Cassie was no different. It surprised me when she asked to sit with Linda, but right away I could see it was the best thing that could have happened.

What a contrast they made! Linda, dark tangles hanging about her slightly grubby pixie face, dressed in something either too small or bought to fit a year from now, and shoes so scuffed and worn they probably would have been rejected by any charity organization. And Cassie all pink and blonde, hair wisping softly over her shoulders. Her clothes obviously came from the best stores, and I could hardly remember her wearing the same outfit more than once or twice.

But they became best friends. They were always involved in intense conversations, giggling and whispering secrets as little girls do, peeking over the seat to make sure no one was listening.

Lately though, the conversation had gotten quieter, the giggles coming less and less frequently. Occasionally, I caught one of them glancing up at me in the overhead mirror.

It puzzled me, the expressions I saw on their faces when I caught them unaware. A nervous frightened look, somehow, like a puppy who knows he's done something wrong, but isn't quite sure what.

Yet, I hadn't really thought anymore about it.

Until now, after the school program.

Daddy's Little Girl

Now I began to put things together that I really didn't want to fit. How slowly and reluctantly Linda walked down the bus aisle in the afternoon. How she nearly always tried to engage me in some inane conversation while she glanced nervously toward her house and then back to Cassie. Her little feet seemed to drag through quicksand as she started up the dirt lane at last, heading for the old, dilapidated farmhouse.

Even Cassie seemed to be affected. The new subdivision where her parents had just built a home was not far down the road, and when I pulled to a stop there, Cassie was often still staring out the window where she'd last seen Linda.

The unease within me was growing, but each night as I watched Cassie walk away from the bus, I was glad that she had a nice home and a loving family to go home to.

I ached for Linda. I prayed that if something really was wrong at home, Cassie would help her tell. Tell someone . . . anyone. For only with the telling would there come help.

It was a bright September morning when I found both little girls standing beside me, their hands tightly clasped. I could hardly breathe as I looked at their pale faces.

"Tell her," Cassie whispered. "Please."

Linda trembled as her lips struggled to form the words.

"It's about what they told us in school," she said. "That we should tell . . ."

It broke my heart to see them standing there, two little babies who knew too much about life. I reached out to Linda. I wanted to hold her, protect her, but when I lifted my hand, she stepped away.

And then with one hesitant sentence, she'd destroyed all I'd ever believed about right and wrong, and good guys and bad guys, and how things are in the world.

"It's Cassie," she said. "Cassie and her daddy need help."

A FATHER AND SON

When I ran into Dan Rawlings at the post office, I thought at first he might just walk right by. Then I decided I just wasn't going to allow that.

"Hi, Dan," I said, stepping in front of him. "How are you?"

A lifelong farmer, Dan was tall and broad and muscular. As a young man, he'd actually made the try-outs for a pro football team, then gave it up to take over the family farm. He was well liked in our farming community; "salt of the earth," his neighbors said, "a man of character." But now his smile was tentative as he gathered his thoughts. He wasn't sure he liked me knowing what I knew.

"OK. Yourself?"

I nodded, searching for a way to ask. And then I just did it.

"How's Robbie?"

He looked off into the distance, at the ceiling, at the floor . . . everywhere but into my eyes. I saw him blink back tears.

"He's fine, I guess. We don't talk much." Then he looked right at me and said firmly, "But at least we talk."

I searched his face for the embarrassment, the all-consuming rage I'd seen there five years ago. It was gone, replaced by a more painful emotion, a mixture of fear and confusion.

It was the same look I'd seen on Robbie Rawlings's face all through his senior year in high school.

A Father and Son

The Rawlings's farm was on my bus route, and Robbie had ridden to school with me since kindergarten. I'd always known him to be a quiet, gentle boy who smiled a lot but was too shy to say much. He was the type of kid who faded into the woodwork and no one cared. I'm sure most of the kids in his class couldn't put a face to his name if they were asked six months after graduation.

Unlike his outgoing father, Rob had never had any athletic aspirations at all. He didn't like being shoved, and he didn't like shoving anyone else. I'd watched his dad try to throw a football to him when he was just a youngster, and even from a distance, I could see how much Rob disliked it.

But he always brought home an excellent report card. Until he got too old to share such things with an adult, he proudly gave me his card to read each grading period. And each time, I was astounded.

I always wondered if it mattered to Dan Rawlings.

I don't know when the word "gay" first came up in the same sentence as Rob's name. A rumor at the grocery store, a whispered statement at the coffee shop. But I knew for sure when Dan found out about his only son.

It was a cold, wind-swept April morning, a few weeks before high-school graduation. When I braked to a stop at the end of the Rawlings's driveway, I could hear the shouting. Rob was waiting for me next to the mailbox, his shoulder-length brown hair whipping about his face. His father was on the porch steps, shirtless on the cold day, leaning over the metal railing. Even from so far away, the rage, the raw agony in Dan's voice sent chills down my back.

"Get out of my sight!" he roared. "Don't you ever think you can come back here!"

He was still shouting when Rob climbed the steps into the bus. I could hear his furious cries over the engine noise as we drove away. My hands were shaking. I glanced up in my overhead mirror, saw the agony on Rob's face as he stared out the window at nothing.

I stopped him before he went down the bus steps as the kids got off at the high school.

"Rob, if I can help . . ." I said. I didn't know what to do, what to say. I saw a touch of a smile around his mouth.

"Thanks," he said. "I don't guess there's much anyone can do." And he walked away. My heart ached for him. For them both.

Now Dan's face twisted in a grimace as he correctly guessed what I was thinking.

"It was a bad scene, wasn't it," he said. "It all caught me by surprise. I never had a clue."

"Kids are good at surprises," I assured him.

Dan sighed. "I guess we should have known in kindergarten when we asked him who was the prettiest one in his class and he said 'James.' " He tried to smile and failed miserably.

"He has a . . . a . . . companion," he continued. The words were torn from his heart. He looked at me in anguish, this hulk of a man who had never known anything but home and family and hard work. In all his life, he'd never found anything he couldn't beat up or shout down and make to his liking. Now he was faced with something he couldn't control, and the helplessness was eating him alive.

But there was hope in his eyes.

"I've been so scared for him," he said, "all the things that go around these days."

I nodded. "The world's a pretty tough place."

Dan took a deep breath, relieved at how the conversation was going. "Anyhow, he wants to come home to visit," he said, rubbing his forehead with a huge, callused hand. "He wants to bring his . . . friend."

He was doing the best he could to understand what he couldn't accept.

I waited. I knew there was more he needed to tell me.

"I don't know," he said finally. "I told him I just need a little more time. Then we'll plan something."

"Well, tell him to be sure to stop by and see me," I said. "I miss him."

Dan looked straight at me, and this time he didn't try to stop the tears tracing down his sun-weathered cheeks.

"So do I," he whispered. "So do I."

THE BEST DAD

"You dummy," the voice behind me said. "No one can do that."

I looked into my overhead rearview mirror and watched little Ryan King nodding. "Oh yes, he did," he shouted. "My dad did!" Ryan was seven, a second-grader. He'd only ridden my bus for a few months, and I didn't know his family. From the sound of the argument, I evidently needed to find out.

Jake Preston, the fifth-grade boy who had started the whole thing, wasn't done. "Your dad didn't win a stock car race and then a golf tournament the next day," Jake said. "You're making it all up, you idiot. I don't think you even have a dad."

"I do too!" Ryan cried, tears welling in his eyes.

"Well, where is he, then?" Jake asked, laughing. "Is he going to come on the Father-Son Day trip tomorrow?"

For weeks, the kids had talked of nothing else. The Father-Son Day was when every kid got to show off his dad to everyone else.

"He . . . he . . . has to work," Ryan stammered. "He's . . . out of town. He works out of town all the time."

"You're such a liar," Jake sneered. The rest of the kids quickly took up a chant. "Ryan's a liar, Ryan's a liar . . ."

Ryan started to cry harder, and I'd had enough. I pulled to the side of the road and braked to a stop. The bus went silent. They all knew they were in trouble as I sat for a moment, looking up into my rearview mirror, trying to get my temper under control. I hated it when any of the kids on my school bus bullied others, but I didn't want to turn into the one doing the bullying.

Finally I unbuckled my seat belt and walked to Ryan. "Making another person cry is not on my list of fun things to do," I said, looking right at Jake and then at all the rest of them. "I don't want to hear any more of this teasing."

"Well, he lies all the time," Jake muttered, avoiding my eyes. "He's always saying things about his dad that aren't true."

"I'm not!" Ryan cried. "I'm not lying. My dad . . ."

"OK," I said to both of them. "That's enough." I took Ryan by the hand and escorted him to the front seat behind me. I knew he'd be relatively safe there.

"It's true," he sniffled. But his voice sounded shaky and hollow even to me. When I looked back at him in my rearview mirror, he was staring out the window, his eyes swollen and red-rimmed—and hopeless.

After I dropped the kids off at the school, I went into the front office. Carl Blake, the grade-school principal, looked through his records. He finally frowned and shook his head. "No father listed on anything we have here," he said. "What's the problem?"

I explained the situation to him and finished by saying, "All of them have been talking about their dads coming to school tomorrow. It's so important to Ryan that all the kids know he's got a dad, just like everyone else. I don't know what to do for him."

"Ah," Carl said. "I see." He looked thoughtful. "I might be able to help," he said with a smile. "Tell you what, I'll meet you in the parking lot this afternoon and see what I can do."

I really didn't have any hopes that Carl could fix the problem. Not unless he could find Ryan's father. And that wasn't likely to happen before the afternoon bus run. But I had no other plan to help the unhappy little second-grader. I knew Carl filled in as the pastor of his small church and was accustomed to counseling and talking to groups. I prayed he could work a miracle.

Carl came out to my bus that afternoon as the kids were getting on to go home. He watched from the sidewalk until they were all in their seats before he stepped up into the bus and stood next to me.

The Best Dad

He waited. The chatter and general commotion gradually died as the kids noticed him. Finally, it was almost quiet, curious whispers the only sound.

"Tomorrow will be our grade-school Father-Son Day trip," he announced, as though each of the kids on the bus wasn't bursting with anticipation. "We're going to have a great time. I'm looking forward to meeting all your dads."

He walked down the aisle, looking at each face. "I know some of your fathers might be unable to attend, and you may have an uncle or an older brother coming with you . . ."

He stopped next to Ryan's seat and stared at him. "And some of you might not have anyone available to come with you for the day." From the back of the bus I heard a snicker. "Yeah, Ryan's dad is too busy winning stock car races and golf tournaments and saving the world," a voice muttered. Giggles ran up and down the bus aisle. Ryan's face turned red. I saw tears come to the edges of his dark eyes again.

"Excuse me?" Carl said, bending closer to look at Ryan. "Are you Ryan King?"

Ryan looked up at him miserably. From the expression on his little face, he wished he was someone else, *anyone* else.

Carl's eyebrows crunched together as he appeared to be concentrating. "I think I know your father," he said.

The giggles ended abruptly. I saw the looks of astonishment on the faces of the kids in the back seats. Even Ryan was mystified, his eyes wide as saucers.

"Yes," Carl said, "I'm sure I know Him. There's a great family resemblance."

Now the silence was deafening. Even the older kids in the back were paying attention.

"I'll bet most of you know Him, too," Carl said, and I could tell he was just getting warmed up. "Ryan's Dad is a pretty talented guy. He can turn water into wine."

I heard the murmurs of disbelief from the little kids, the uncomfortable shuffling in the back of the bus from the older ones. But Carl wasn't done. "And that's just a little thing. He has raised people from the dead, and He's made blind people see."

He looked from face to face to face, making eye contact with each child. "He's the Ruler of the world, and He holds your life in his Hands. If you don't know Him, you might want to say 'hello' today. He'll be standing right next to Ryan."

He knelt on one knee next to Ryan's seat. "Don't you know, Ryan?" he said, his voice just above a whisper that rang through the bus like a microphone. "You're a child of God."

For once, Ryan was speechless. He watched Carl's departing back and sat quietly in his seat as we pulled away from the grade school. The little kids were wide-eyed and spellbound with the information, the big ones shamed into silence.

I glanced up into my overhead mirror and smiled when I saw the look on Ryan's face. It was wonder. It was hope.

Section 2

Prayers and Promises

LIFE LESSON

"If that's the way you feel, then get lost!" Jenny Marcus snapped as she walked down the school-bus steps with Adam Rialto. Then she stormed into the high school alone. Adam followed at a distance, anger reddening his face.

Even though they'd both ridden my school bus since kindergarten, Adam and Jenny weren't included in my list of favorite people. They'd been dating steadily throughout their junior year, and I was just a little sick of them both.

Adam, in particular, got under my skin. A strikingly handsome boy, he had sultry brown eyes and a gorgeous mop of dark hair that hung in waves to his shoulders. He was the football team quarterback, star forward in basketball, president of the student council, homecoming king with Jenny as his queen, and on and on. A general all-around idol of sorts.

An *all around jerk*, I thought privately. He made no attempt to be a nice guy; he just lived on his glory, sure that everyone would pay court to his superiority. His teasing of the less popular kids on the bus was out-and-out mean. I did what little I could to keep him quiet without making it worse for the objects of his torment.

Jenny pretty much went along with whatever devilment Adam planned. And of course, she had her own entourage. Both boys and girls fawned on her, anxious to be a part of her group.

Life Lesson

So more than anything, I was amused when they had their little tiff on the bus. All was not perfect in the kingdom, it seemed. I had to hide my smile that afternoon when they ignored each other as they boarded the bus.

Then I felt a cold chill when Adam slid into the seat beside Nan Radford.

Poor Nan. Such a sweet little girl. She was shy and quiet, her huge blue eyes never making direct contact, her heavy blond hair swinging about her face like a curtain. As pretty as she was, she was the kind of kid who faded into the woodwork, someone whose name would come up at the ten-year reunion and everyone would look puzzled. The boys hadn't seemed too interested in her, and I saw the wonder in her eyes when she looked up at Adam.

He put his arm across the back of the seat and smiled down at her. The cold chill went all the way to my toes. I wanted to tell her to run, to get as far away from Adam as she could. But I was just the bus driver, and I had to swallow the words, gritting my teeth to keep from telling Adam what I thought.

Nan and Adam became an item the next few weeks. He sat with her, held her hand when they walked to and from school, opened the doors for her—all in direct sight of Jenny, I noticed.

But Nan didn't seem to care. The stars never left her eyes.

Until the high-schoolers started to whisper and stare at her three months later. The rumors were flying, wild and vicious. And unfortunately, they were true.

On a frosty winter morning, Nan walked up the bus steps as though she were walking into the mouth of hell. Her face was pale, her eyes dark circles of pain. She slid into the seat with Adam, and I couldn't make out her urgent whispers.

I didn't have any trouble at all, though, hearing Adam's laugh.

"What do you expect me to do?" he said. "How do I even know it's mine?" He stood up and moved to another seat, leaving Nan huddled in her corner alone. In my overhead mirror, I saw him wink at his friends and fold his arms in the classic "strong man" position. The other boys giggled and snorted crudely.

I heard other bits of the conversation. "Hey, big stud!" "Way to go!" And then a more quietly spoken, "What's she going to do?"

"Who knows?" Adam shrugged to show how little he cared. "It's her problem, not mine."

I was a heartbeat away from hitting the brakes and storming to the back seats. Not that I expected Adam to play the hero and get married at sixteen to a fifteen-year-old bride. But I didn't think it would be unreasonable for him to shoulder at least half the responsibility for the life he'd helped create. Unfortunately, I was only the bus driver, and it wasn't in my power to solve life problems. I took a deep breath and gripped the steering wheel more tightly.

Adam, in the meantime, moved back into Jenny's seat. I ached for Nan as she watched the pair walk hand and hand into school. When Jenny looked back over her shoulder, a satisfied smile on her face, Nan seemed to shrink even more, her face pale and haunted.

I didn't see Nan after that week. Someone said she was being homeschooled until the baby was born. I listened to Adam's bragging, heard the pride and arrogance in his voice.

"Yeah, it's mine, all right," he said to his friends who stared up at him in open-mouthed wonder. "She was easy." He winked at the girls across the aisle. They giggled.

Something very close to hate gnawed at my soul. I was a breath away from telling the kid what I thought. Too bad the words I wanted to use were strictly forbidden by the bus drivers' manual. How unfair that adults have to play by the rules.

On a beautiful warm spring day, I stopped at Adam's driveway and watched him strut to the bus. I knew before he even opened his mouth.

"She had it," I heard him tell the guys in the back. "A boy. Weighed eight pounds."

Everyone was suitably impressed. I heard words like "Wow, what a man!" "Big stud!" And other comments, even more obscene.

It was more than I could take. I reached for my seat belt and stood up, intending to tear every one of them limb from limb. But Adam's next comment made me hesitate.

"I'm going to the hospital tonight to see it," he said.

I sat back down in my seat. Something inside told me to take a deep breath and wait.

The next morning I knew why.

Life Lesson

I barely recognized Adam as he walked down his driveway to meet the bus. His face was drawn . . . aged a hundred years, I thought, his eyes dark and puffy. He walked up the steps slowly, avoiding my gaze, and slid into the first open seat.

"Well?" one of his buddies leaned over the back of the seat and questioned him. "Did you go? Did you see it?"

While I watched in my overhead mirror, Adam leaned back in his seat, staring at the ceiling.

"It's a baby," he said so quietly I could barely hear. "A baby!" He repeated it, a sound of wonder making the words tremble. "He has brown eyes and dark hair and broad hands, just like me." He spread his fingers and examined them for a long time, then shifted in his seat and stared across the aisle at his friends. His face twisted with a confused mixture of adult comprehension and child's pain.

"He's my *son*," he said, his voice cracking in a way I hadn't heard since he'd left junior high. "*My son*."

His next words were torn from his heart. "We named him Jeremy," he whispered. "And we gave him away."

The silence was overwhelming. Not one kid moved or said a word. Quietly, I put the bus in gear, glad that I hadn't interfered. I prayed maybe a few of these kids had learned what a tough game life was when at last you were forced to play by grown-up rules.

EYES OF A STRANGER

I saw Laura today. In the eyes of a stranger, I saw her spirit, her sense of fun and happiness. I felt the pain in my heart soften, and I smiled, remembering . . .

In my many years of driving a school bus, I'd met every kind of kid. A few, of course, I didn't want to run into as adults. But there were many I was sure would go on to do great things in the world. Laura Stratton was one of the special ones. Her parents, Don and Liz, had been friends of mine for years, and I'd welcomed their daughter onto the bus as a kindergartener. Over the years I'd watched her grow not only in size but in spirit and heart. Such a kind, gentle soul. I don't think she ever had an enemy in the whole school. She was a pal to everyone. As a high-school junior, she'd already decided she wanted to become a psychologist, because friends felt they could confide in her. "And I'm good at listening," she said, grinning.

But her greatest love was singing. From kindergarten on, she was chosen to sing the lead at the school music festivals. She eagerly sang in her church choir, and as she matured, she was asked to perform at weddings and funerals and everything in between.

"I like making people happy," she told me once. "And sometimes my singing can do that. I like the looks on people's faces when they listen to me."

I knew I'd forever remember how she looked that last day she rode my school bus. So small and delicate, she seemed much younger than her sixteen years. Her long, brown hair framed her delicate, heart-shaped face, while her wayward bangs wisped across her forehead. She fought the stubborn bangs every morning with a curling iron. "They always win," she sighed, on more than one occasion.

Laura had just passed her driver's test, and this was her last ride on my school bus. "It's kind of sad," she said, trying not to smile. "I'll miss riding the bus."

I repressed my smile, too. I knew she was lying to make me feel better. Like any teen with a new driver's license, she couldn't wait to get behind the wheel of her newly acquired car, the old silver four-door her dad had given her.

On Friday, the second day of her junior year, a half-hour before sunrise, Laura started her car and backed out of the driveway. Typical of her, she'd volunteered to drive a friend to school for early morning chorus practice. A block away from home, she pulled out onto the highway. We never knew if she misjudged the speed of the truck coming toward her or simply didn't see it. Her dad heard the crash and ran outside. He found his daughter slumped unconscious on the front seat of the wrecked car. The doctors pronounced her dead the following morning.

And then they took Don and Liz Stratton aside to ask if they'd consider donating Laura's organs.

I knew the Strattons well enough to realize how hard it was for them. But they knew immediately what they were going to do. They were sure it was exactly what Laura would have wanted, and they didn't hesitate.

Surgical teams scrambled. Operating rooms were readied. Tissue samples were cross-matched with names in a vast database of desperately ill people waiting for transplants. Early Sunday morning, when the rest of us were just beginning to deal with the pain of Laura's death, her parents were told that five people had been successfully transplanted with their daughter's organs. Liz and Don tried to take comfort in knowing how happy Laura would be, how proud she would have been to save these five strangers who had been facing their own certain deaths. The small measure of comfort was short-lived. Laura was gone from them forever.

For me, at least, there was no comfort. One day she'd been sitting in the bus seat behind me, grinning and chatting with all the nearby kids. Forty-eight hours later, I was told I'd never see her again. I tried to tell myself that some good had come of the tragedy, but deep inside I felt it was unfair for another person to be continuing with his or her life because Laura's had ended.

Days after the funeral, I stopped by the Strattons' house to share some "Laura" stories with them. We talked, and after a while, they took me into her room. We stood there silently, searching for her in a hundred mementos. Schoolbooks, clothes, pictures on the wall. The Strattons hadn't moved a thing. Don picked up a fuzzy teddy bear on the bed, and I saw his hands trembling.

"I shouldn't have let her drive," he muttered, clutching the bear to his chest. Liz touched his arm.

"It wasn't your fault," she said.

They huddled together in the doorway, trying to find a way past the grief. There was nothing I could do to ease their pain. Or my own.

After a moment, Liz stepped back and looked at me. "We received the most wonderful letter," she said shakily. "The woman who . . . who . . ." She couldn't get the words out. I waited while she took a deep breath. "The woman who was transplanted with Laura's lungs."

She glanced at Don, wondering if this was something she should share with me. He nodded.

"Her name is Kay," Liz continued. "As soon as she's recovered, she and her husband want to meet us."

My heart turned over. How hard it had to be to meet the person who was alive because Laura had died. How would they look into her face?

It was months later when I stopped at Laura's driveway again. I'd been lost in thought that late September morning. Thoughts of renewal, thoughts of things past. I'd seen Laura's face in the mist over the meadows, in the reflection in my windshield. I hadn't stopped the bus at the Strattons' since the day Laura quit riding, so I was startled when I saw the four people standing there.

I was glad the bus was empty as I took a deep breath, turned on the overhead flashers, and braked to a stop. I opened the folding door and waited, my heart pounding fiercely. I knew who the other couple had to be.

Liz Stratton put her hand on the door and looked up at me. Tears ran down her cheeks, but she was smiling, and her eyes were bright. "I thought you might like to meet them," she said. "This is Kay and her husband, Gary."

I looked down at the middle-aged woman and felt my heart turn over. She was small, like Laura, but with gray-streaked, black hair. She held out her arms to me. With shaking hands, I unfastened my seat belt and walked down the steps to hug her. I could feel her body trembling, too.

Then I stepped back and looked into her face, into her eyes. It blew my mind away. Someone was talking, but I couldn't make out the words. I could only stare into Kay's eyes. Then I turned to Liz Stratton. Did she see it? Did we all see it?

Liz nodded and smiled at me, tears brimming in her eyes. Of course she saw it. After a moment, I started to hear what Kay was saying to me.

"I was supposed to die," she said. "I'd ruined my lungs with years of cigarettes. I used to love to sing in the church choir, but at the end, I couldn't breathe without oxygen, much less sing."

She started to cry then and turned toward the Strattons. "Now we sing together in the choir, Gary and I," she said. "Laura—and her mom and dad—gave me my life back."

I climbed back up the bus steps and smiled as I started the engine and shifted into gear. Nothing would ever take away the pain of losing Laura, but now I finally understood what good she and her parents had done. The essence of Laura was still with us. It was something to hold on to, something to soften the edges of the pain.

I saw Laura today. She lives still in the eyes of a stranger.

NEVER STOP, MIKE

"Mrs. Gulley, stop!"

The shout from the back of the school bus made my hair stand on end. I hit the brakes hard, and the wheels slid in the snow and slush on the country road.

I gritted my teeth, pulled over to the side, and repeated to myself, as I had many times that winter, "Mike Fuller is not a bad kid!" It was just a week before Christmas break, and I knew it was going to take all my willpower to retain my spirit of goodwill with this boy.

Then I unfastened my seat belt, walked to the back, and stood next to Mike's seat.

"Can you explain why you had to shout, almost causing an accident?" I said, somehow keeping my words calm.

The tall, dark-headed sophomore looked up at me, his brown eyes wide with shock and innocence.

"I had to shut Tony's window," he said, a note of hurt in his voice. "And you said it's against the rules for us to stand up when the bus is moving."

I sighed, trying to unclench my teeth. "Mike," I said. "If you don't quit annoying me, I'm going to have to take you in to see Principal Anderson."

He raised his eyebrows pleasantly, pretending not to understand. "Annoy you? Why, Mrs. Gulley, do you think I'd ever intentionally do anything to make you mad?" I opened my mouth, finally losing control, fully intending to yell at him, but he beat me to the punch . . . as usual.

"Do you know you're even more beautiful when you're angry?"

The little kids all giggled. I felt my face flame. I shut my mouth and went back to my seat. What was I going to do with this boy?

Mike had been a quiet little kid all through grade school. It was as a high-school freshman that he'd changed. He didn't do anything really bad . . . just things designed to drive me crazy. He delighted in crawling under the seats to the grade-school section of the bus and teasing the little kids until they screamed. Sometimes he'd eat sunflower seeds and scatter handfuls of hulls in the back seats. When I ordered him to clean up the mess, he always obeyed cheerfully, but it didn't stop him from the next disaster. And the next.

I was so lost in my irritated thoughts and feelings that I didn't see the person standing at the next driveway. "Mrs. Gulley! Stop!" Mike shouted again. The woman waved frantically at me. Tammy Garcia, our mail delivery person.

My face red, I slammed on the brakes, and this time the rear tires slid just a foot or two. As I swung open the folding door, I fumed inside at my lack of attention—and Mike's big mouth.

The agony on the woman's face made me quickly forget my problems. "Mrs. Garcia," I said, "I'm sorry. I didn't mean . . ."

The small, dark-haired woman shook her head, tears brimming in her brown eyes. She stepped inside the bus and leaned close to me. "I've done something so stupid," she whispered. "I set my purse on top of my delivery car when I left to do my route yesterday." Her voice was thick with remorse. "I didn't remember until I looked for my purse this morning."

She looked down the bus aisle at the kids. "It had . . . it had all our Christmas money in it. Cash. My whole last week's check." The tears spilled out and trickled down her cheeks.

I knew she was a single mom, working long hours as a mail delivery person to support her two preschoolers.

"Have you checked the roads?" I asked.

She nodded. "I drove and drove," she said. "I backtracked everywhere. I couldn't find it. I thought it might help to tell the bus drivers and ask if they'd watch for it."

"I'll keep an eye out," I said, trying to be reassuring. But I thought it was unlikely the purse would be found after a day. Especially since it contained a large amount of cash.

The kids behind me had grown very quiet, and I knew they were listening.

I looked up in the overhead mirror. "Everyone be on the lookout for a purse on the road," I said.

Mrs. Garcia waved as we pulled away.

I'd picked up my last rider and we'd turned onto the main black-top back into town when the by-now familiar shout made me grit my teeth.

"Stop, Mrs. Gulley! Stop!" I looked up into the overhead mirror, ready to stare daggers at Mike, but a chorus of voices joined his. "There it is, Mrs. Gulley! Stop! Stop!" I hit the brakes and one more time pulled to the side. The bus was still rolling when Mike appeared at my elbow. He didn't wait for me to pull open the door, just grabbed the lever and did it himself. He climbed down into the ditch and pulled the black purse out of the weeds.

My heart filled with hope, but as Mike carried it back to the bus, I saw him look inside and shake his head.

"It's empty," he said, showing me.

I sighed. I'd hoped maybe . . .

"I'll return it to Mrs. Garcia," I said. But I knew it wasn't the purse she needed. I hated to tell her the money was gone.

After I dropped everyone off at their respective schools, I decided to leave the purse on the bus and give it to Mrs. Garcia on my way past her house that afternoon. And I decided something else. I slipped a twenty dollar bill into the black purse. It wasn't much, but it was all I could afford.

At the end of the school day, I once again picked up all my riders, and we headed back out into the country to deliver them home. When I stopped at Tammy Garcia's driveway, I reached down for the purse. It was gone.

I took a deep breath and looked up into the overhead mirror, my heart racing. Could someone have stolen it again? I knew it had been there when I'd started loading passengers. Then I saw an object being passed from person to person toward the front of the bus.

Never Stop, Mike

Jason Reilly, a first-grader just behind me, took it and leaned forward. "Here it is, Mrs. Gulley." He handed the purse to me, but something was different. It was round and fat. Slowly, I pulled the clasp open and felt my heart turn over. It was filled with a jumble of dollar bills.

I turned around, speechless. The busload of kids stared back at me, smiling, looking embarrassed. The little ones in front giggled with excitement.

"Where did this come from?" I finally managed to get the words out.

For a moment, there was silence on the bus. Then Jason grinned shyly.

"It was Mike's idea," he said. "He went around all day at school and had people give money."

"Mike?" I said stupidly. I almost said, "Mike who?"

"Yeah," one of the others added. "He put in the most money too."

"Mike," I said. "Come up here."

Looking uncomfortable for the first time in his life, Mike sauntered to the front. I raised my eyebrows, a silent question.

Mike avoided my stare and shrugged. "I had some money saved up to buy speakers for my stereo, but the old ones are pretty good."

Then he looked right at me and for the first time, his eyes were serious. In that instant, I saw the man he was to become, and I felt myself smile.

"Hey, I know I'm a jerk," he said, smiling back. "But I never pretended to be a Scrooge." He pulled Jason's cap down over his eyes and shoved him back into the corner of the seat.

"Merry Christmas," he said cheerfully, and turned to walk away.

"Mike, stop!" I said. He glanced back, surprised. Then I saw the panic on his face as he realized what I was going to do.

"Oh no," he said. "Not a hug! You'll ruin my image . . . You'll . . ."

But it was too late. I wrapped my arms around him as the other kids laughed and applauded.

"Merry Christmas," I said to him and to all of them, trying not to cry. "Merry Christmas!"

TIME TO HEAL

The small boy stood in the bus aisle, his face scarlet with rage, his hands clawing at the face of the high-school boy who was trying to move him out of the way.

"Al and Lonnie!" I shouted, pulling the bus to the side of the road. "Stop that and sit down." I was talking to the air. They continued to struggle as I turned the key off and stalked back to the commotion.

Alan Simmons finally gripped the dark-headed little Tasmanian devil by the arms and pinned him into the seat.

"Mrs. Gulley, I swear," he panted. "I swear I didn't do anything. I just told him to move."

"I know," I said. "It's OK. Let him go." Alan stepped back, and Lonnie Davis, just a fourth-grader, roared out of the seat like a young lion cub. I stepped between him and the object of his unreasonable fury—and was nearly bowled over.

"Lonnie, calm down," I said, trying to hold back the small boy. When at last he saw he couldn't squeeze around me in the narrow bus aisle, he threw himself into a seat, his lower lip stuck out, arms crossed across his chest. I thought he resembled a dark-headed troll. And just about as likeable.

"This time I'm going to call your mom," I said, feeling my head start to pound.

"She's not my mom," he sputtered, his face twisted with anger.

"Whatever," I told him. "I'm not putting up with this kind of behavior anymore."

"Whatever," he mimicked me, wrinkling his nose. "And I don't care if I ride this stupid bus anyway."

I resisted the urge to shove him out the door and make his wish come true.

It was a bad idea from the start. I could have told Elaine Claude that, but I'm just the bus driver, and who was I to tell her not to adopt her sister's ten-year-old son?

Lonnie came from the heart of the city, raised by a dad who no doubt kept him around for the additional welfare money. At one point, the pair were living in a van on the city streets. When the boy was six, the dad tried to hold up a convenience store and went to prison. Because Lonnie's mom had never wanted him, the six-year-old went to foster care, which didn't last long. Even those most hardened to this kind of kid couldn't put up with his temper and tantrums and street-wise mouth. He was shuffled from institutions to foster homes and back, until Elaine couldn't stand it anymore.

"What else can I do?" she lamented. "There's no other place for him. He's my nephew."

As I dragged Lonnie off the bus and into Principal Anderson's office, I wondered if Elaine was second-guessing her decision.

Principal Anderson was on the phone almost before I'd shut the door behind us. He'd dealt with Lonnie before. Elaine was there in just a few minutes, as though she'd been expecting the call. And, in fact, I'm sure it was no surprise.

A slight, gray-headed woman in her forties, she looked as though a strong gust of wind could topple her. When she turned to Lonnie, the expression on her face was a mixture of helplessness and bewilderment and sadness. I wondered what was in her heart.

"Mrs. Claude, Lonnie had a problem on the bus this morning," Mr. Anderson began. He explained to her what had happened, and she seemed to get smaller and more pale with every word.

"Oh, Lonnie," was all she said.

"Perhaps we'd better send him home for the day," Principal Anderson concluded. "He'll be suspended from the bus for a week, school policy for fighting. And an additional five days of detentions."

"Good," Lonnie said, jumping to his feet. "I don't ever want to ride that dumb bus again. She's a stupid driver." Hate and anger and something—something I didn't understand—glowed from his eyes like coals in a dying fire.

Elaine reached for him, but he ducked away.

"I never wanted to go to this school," he ranted on. "I didn't want to come here."

"Sweetheart, don't . . ." she pleaded, holding her hands out to him.

"I hate you," he screamed at her. "I want to go back with my dad. I want my mom."

Elaine's voice didn't change. "Your dad's in jail," she said. "We don't know where your mom is."

"Then send me back," Lonnie shouted. His face crumbled, and he started to sob. "I don't want to live in your stupid house. I don't want to live with you anymore."

The pain in Elaine's pale eyes was liquid, alive. But her voice was strong as she did exactly the right thing, something I know I could never—would never—have done.

She reached out and gathered the small boy into her arms.

"It's OK, Lonnie; we're going to get through this," she said, her words as gentle as the hand she stroked his hair with. "Don't you understand? I'm not going to leave you. Not ever. We're going to stay together, and we're going to be OK."

For a moment, the tough little kid struggled against her. Then his arms went around her waist and held her in a death grip. I could see his shoulders shaking.

Elaine's smile was trembling too as she looked at me.

And suddenly I knew I'd been wrong about her decision. She'd known what she was doing all along. The damage to this child went beyond his heart, deep into his very soul. She knew the only cure was love.

"We'll be back tomorrow," she said. And with her arm about his shoulders, holding him close against her side, she took her son home.

STICKS AND STONES

"You stupid jerk!" The tone of the voice made the hair stand up on the back of my neck. "What an idiot. Do you have sawdust for brains?"

I took my foot off the gas and looked up in the overhead mirror of my school bus, searching back through the rows of kids to find the one speaking. It didn't take long.

"Danny!" It was a tone I reserved for special occasions, and every kid on the bus knew what it meant.

Everyone, it seemed, but Danny Marshall.

Short and too stocky for a ten-year-old, Danny's attitude and manners were sometimes more befitting those of an elderly grinch. He didn't say much, but when he chose to speak, it was almost always to belittle someone, call attention to an error, or make the person cry.

"This retard says we don't have school on Friday," Danny complained, pointing at Jeremy Allen, a kindergartner in an opposite seat. Danny's pinched, sour little face looked even more pouty than usual. His black hair hung down on his forehead in bangs cut so thick they rolled over his heavy gold-rimmed glasses and threatened to shove them down his nose. Poking the wire rims back into place with his index finger, he stared defiantly at me.

I sighed.

"He's just confusing this week with next," I said. "We're off a week from Friday for parent-teacher conferences. It's not a capital offense, Danny, to make a mistake."

Danny shrugged, his thin lips tipped down at the corners. Evidently, there was no mercy in his soul for mistakes.

"He's dumb," he said.

"I am not!" Jeremy shouted. Big tears rolled down his cheeks.

"You dumb, stupid crybaby," Danny taunted.

I pulled the bus to the side of the road, shut off the key, and stalked back to where Danny was sitting.

"Come on," I told him, my face inches from his. My fingers itched to grab him and shake him just to see his head rattle. "I have a nice empty seat for you in the front."

"Why?" he cried. "What did I do?" He continued to complain as he followed me to the front seat where I put troublemakers; he threw himself into the corner, arms crossed tightly over his chest, lower lip jutted out.

I sighed again as I started the bus and headed down the road. Same old story, different morning.

More than once I'd taken Danny in to talk to Mr. Anderson, the grade-school principal, and the results were always pretty much the same; though the fifth-grader grudgingly kept his mouth shut for a time, it wasn't long before he lashed out at someone. He never ever hit or used physical violence of any kind. But the things he said, the words he used, often hit harder than a fist, cut deeper than a knife. He was a master at hurting others' feelings, an expert at cruelty far beyond his years.

As I steered the bus into the grade-school parking lot, I thought about what I should do. Danny was out of control. It had to stop.

"Danny, stay in your seat," I ordered. I opened the door, and when the last child had hopped down the stairs, I took Danny to the principal's office. Mr. Anderson raised his eyebrows as we entered.

"Well, Danny," he said with a sigh. "I remember telling you I'd have to call your parents if you continued to get into trouble on the bus."

Danny looked up at me, at Principal Anderson. "Please," he begged, more quietly than I'd ever heard him speak. "Please, I'll be good. Please. Don't call my dad." He was trembling, his big eyes bright and liquid.

"It's too late, Danny," Principal Anderson said. "You had your chance." He reached for the phone and started dialing.

Sticks and Stones

The man who strode into the office ten minutes later was a tall version of his son, black hair, big dark eyes, thin pouty lips, and a face that seemed to find nothing amusing about the world. He shut the door behind him.

And took my breath away as he grabbed Danny by the shirtfront. "You retarded little toad!" he snarled through clenched teeth. "What did I tell you about getting into trouble at school, you idiot? Do you know I'll be late to work now because of your stupidity?"

Danny's teeth were chattering, his eyes huge and frightened. "I . . . I'm sorry," he stuttered. "I didn't . . ."

"Oh, you're sorry! Well, your mother and I are sorry, too. Sorry we ever brought you home from the hospital the day you were born." The boy's father shoved him back into the chair. "If you can't use your miserable peabrain, then at least keep your big mouth shut."

I couldn't believe what was happening. I sat up in my chair, looking with horror at Mr. Anderson.

"Ah, . . . Mr. Marshall," the principal said, rising to his feet behind the desk. "I really don't think Danny needs to be spoken to like that. Perhaps we could send him to class now, and you and I could discuss this."

"Sure, send the little dummy to class," the man said, turning his back on his son. "I can't stand the sight of him."

Mr. Anderson nodded at me. I grabbed Danny by the hand and fled into the hall, slamming the office door behind us.

My heart was pounding against my ribcage as we walked toward the fifth-grade rooms, my mind racing in a hundred directions. I still couldn't believe what I'd heard.

Beside me, for once in his life, Danny was silent.

We reached the door of his room, and he stopped. He wiped his face, blew his nose on his sleeve, and looked up at me.

And what I saw at last was not just a troublemaker, not a mean, mouthy fifth-grader who delighted in verbally abusing anyone who dared come near. I looked into the shattered soul of a small, helpless being who needed desperately to be loved.

So I tried the one method of discipline I hadn't thought of. I knelt down, put my arms around his shaking shoulders, and hugged him while he sobbed.

THE LIST

My stupid list. Why did I even bother?

I braked my school bus to a stop at the high school and shut the engine off, then turned and ripped the piece of paper from the wall beside me. It was quiet on the bus. The kids behind me knew they were in trouble. And they knew why.

"Does anyone ever read this?" I asked, holding the paper up.

No response. What did I expect?

I put up a different list every year. "Rules to live by," I call them. This year number one was, "Say one nice thing to your mom." Number two was, "Give your teacher a compliment." It was number five that I was interested in. "Be a friend to someone who needs one." I stabbed at the list with my finger. "Do any of you know what this says?"

No one looked.

"What gives you the right to make life miserable for someone else?" I fumed. "Do any of you have a clue what it's like to get on this bus every morning and face brats who have nothing better to do than make someone feel bad?"

I looked at the leaders of the pack: Jennie Schmidt, Brett Jackson, Ryan Fedders, and maybe Sarah Blake. None of them was a troublemaker, but they'd gone down a major step in my estimation this past year.

All because of Tommy Flynn.

The List

When Tommy and his mother moved into our district, I'd heard they were poor. When he'd stepped into the bus that first morning and looked at me, his thin lips curving into a shy smile, I knew the rumors were true.

He was small, frail looking; his pale blue eyes too big for the pinched, drawn face. His shaggy hair and worn clothes weren't those of a fashion rebel—he dressed that way from necessity.

I felt the stares from the back; the whispers a little—a lot—too loud. I hated to send him back there.

"Hi, I'm Tom Flynn," he said, his voice so quiet I had to lean over to hear.

"Hi, I'm Tom Flynn," a high-pitched, whiny voice from the back mimicked him. Both of us pretended not to notice.

"I'm glad to meet you, Tom," I said. Then I hesitated, looking up into the overhead mirror. He understood.

"In the back?"

"You can sit here with the little kids if you like."

"That's OK," he said. "Got to get it over with sooner or later."

This gentle boy had been in new schools before—probably every time the rent was behind. In the overhead mirror, I watched him walk to the back.

Jennie Schmidt wrinkled her nose and scattered her books across the seat. One by one, the rest of them did the same.

"One of you move over," I said. Then I added in a tone I reserved for special occasions, "Now!"

"O-o-oh, bus driver's pet," someone snickered. But they moved.

Pink patches on his cheeks, Tom sat down. I wanted to strangle every one of the back-of-the-bus crowd.

It didn't get any better. I kept my mouth shut, let Tom fight it through on his own. I hoped one of them would show a little compassion, but it soon became apparent that nothing was going to change. They teased, taunted, and made fun. Through it all, Tom was quiet and withdrawn.

Today, Tom hadn't been waiting outside his ramshackle farmhouse. So, when I reached the school, I delivered my furious speech.

Afterward, all I saw were impatient glances, shuffling papers, eyes rolling with mock disgust. I crumpled my list into a ball and threw it into the trash container as I reached for the door handle.

Jan Adams, the school counselor, was standing outside. "Tom Flynn is sick," she said. I could tell by her expression that it wasn't a little cold and fever. "He's in Trinity Hospital," she added. "You might want to tell your kids."

I was in Tommy's room when some of them came to see him. Funny, they were as pale as he was. They sat next to him . . . tried to make small talk—to make themselves feel better, of course. Tommy tried to comfort *them*.

He died a month later. We found out he'd been diagnosed with leukemia just before he'd moved to our town.

For a long time, it was hard for me to talk to the kids in the back. Then I noticed something going on.

For days, I watched the high-schoolers putting their heads together, whispering, glancing my way. No grins and giggles. Serious stuff. When I looked into the overhead mirror, they pretended to be doing nothing.

As I stopped at the high school one morning, Brett stood and leaned across the aisle to talk to a middle-school boy. "Brett? What's the holdup?" I called.

Startled, Brett jumped. Pennies, dimes, and quarters clattered to the floor and rolled under the seats and to the front of the bus, some falling into the step well. The bus grew quiet as the last of the coins clattered and clicked and stopped.

Dark eyes big with anticipation, Brett knelt and began raking coins into a pile.

"What's going on?" I kept my voice as level as I could.

Brett glanced back at his partners in crime. They were silent. Finally he shrugged.

"It's number eight," he said.

What? What was this kid talking about?

"We had a lot of trouble with number five, so we thought we'd try number eight."

He pulled a crumpled bit of paper from his pocket and held it out. The list. I smoothed the paper, my fingers shaking.

Number eight. "Do something nice for someone and don't let

anyone know." I looked up. My confusion must have shown on my face.

Brett shrugged again. "Tom's mother couldn't afford a tombstone," he said.

I looked at them, Brett and Jennie and Ryan and Sarah. Saw the guilt and sorrow in their eyes.

Then I went back to my seat and taped the crumpled piece of paper back to the wall.

A MOMENT IN TIME

The air is crisp and clean with the dryness of late fall, . . . cool, even, while the sun lies warm on my arm and shoulder and the side of my face next to the window. My school-bus engine rumbles; the bus bumps and rocks down the dusty gravel road. The kids behind me stare out the windows, silent. Silent as death.

A morning like any other. A morning like no other. A mourning.

Children have killed children. And although it didn't happen in our small school district, we've forever left behind the notion that it couldn't.

Why? The question is so loud inside my head I can't imagine the kids in the front seats didn't hear. *Why, in the name of all that's perceived to be innocent and good, did You allow this to happen?*

It's a question for God.

I wait, listening to the motor grind up the hill to Cassie Ortega's driveway. God doesn't answer. I feel angry and alone.

Cassie and her mom are standing at the end of the driveway. Cassie is a thin, leggy second-grader with cotton candy blond hair and brilliant blue eyes, a smaller version of her young mother. I flip the switch to start the overhead flashers and brake the bus to a halt. Mrs. Ortega looks up as I open the door in a swirl of dust. She tightens her hold on Cassie's shoulders and tries to smile. I see my thoughts reflected in the dark blue pools of her eyes.

And I know what she wants from me.

A Moment in Time

A promise. A guarantee that if she releases her tenuous hold on this small being she loves with all her heart and entrusts her to my care, I will protect her child and keep her from all harm.

It's a promise I want badly to give. But as Mrs. Ortega and I stare at each other in the brilliant haze of the quiet November morning, we both know it's a promise neither of us can make.

She and I know and understand that even though either of us would die without question for our children, we can't guarantee what tomorrow will bring. Or today, or even the next hour.

The knowing doesn't make life any easier. With the reluctance of a drowning person turning loose of a life vest, Mrs. Ortega releases her hold on Cassie's jacket. The eight-year-old skips up the bus steps, oblivious to the terror in the hearts of the adults who are responsible for her.

I close the doors and put the bus in gear, moving slowly down the country road. In my overhead mirror, I see Mrs. Ortega wrap her arms around her body in a self-hug as she stares after the bus.

I'm so lost in my thoughts, the squabble behind me has reached epic proportions before I realize what's going on.

"Give it back!" Cassie shouts to the older boy behind her. She's on her feet in the seat, hanging over the back.

"Cassie, sit down," I say, more sharply than I intend. There's no response. The shouting gets louder, and I pull the bus to the side of the road, braking to a stop.

By now, Cassie is sobbing. A paper is torn to pieces, scattered in the aisle, and Jason, the fourth-grade tease, is looking innocent.

"It's a picture for my teacher," Cassie wails. "I hate you!" she screams at Jason. "I'm going to get my daddy's gun and kill you!"

The moment is frozen in time. From the back of the bus, one of the older kids moans as though she's been struck. The world has gone somewhere God never intended, and now even the least ones know the words.

I put my arms around Cassie and hold her close to me. *"Don't,"* I whisper. *"Don't."* The words are a plea to God as much as to the small helpless being in my grasp.

Her sobbing fades. I chastise Jason. We make arrangements for Cassie to draw another picture. The moment is past. For now.

But the fear burns bright in my heart, in my soul. Like Cassie, I feel helpless to stop what's happening in the world. Things that are happening to our children. Everything far beyond my control.

And so today I do the one small thing I can do, all that's within my power. As they file off the bus at the grade school, I smile at each young face.

"Take care," I say. "Have a nice day."

And as they walk through the doors into our small country school, where such unspeakable atrocities could never (*"please, God, never"*) happen, I say a prayer for them.

UNDERSTANDING

I braked my school bus to a stop at the country crossroads and looked with disbelief at the building standing just a few yards out into the dried, dusty-yellow cornfield. The kids behind me were staring too. For a moment the bus was silent.

Then: "They're going to die for this." The quiet voice was clear and certain and filled with rage. I shivered on the warm fall morning, contemplating the implications of what I was seeing.

There was profanity—vile words and crude drawings—scrawled on the old corn crib from one end to the other; paint cans and stiff brushes lay strewn in the grass and corn stubble. And right in the middle of it all stood a group of unfamiliar high-school age kids, eyes wide, hands clenched tightly around dripping paint brushes.

For the first time in as long as I'd lived in our small farming community, someone had dared breach the unspoken law among area schools. Not only was the building considered ours alone, a place where senior classes scribbled what they perceived as witty and wise for future classes to view and marvel at, but profanity, anything even remotely off-color, was strictly taboo.

"They're from Spring Hill," another voice growled. A murmur of general agreement went through the bus.

"Let's burn 'em," someone else said. I looked up but couldn't put a face to the threat.

Every school district has at least one particularly hated rival. Spring Hill was ours. What had started out as a healthy, friendly rivalry had somehow degenerated over the years to a bitter and hateful relationship.

Things happened. Off-the-field skirmishes at football games, eggs thrown at windows in the middle of the night, even nasty names scribbled on the side of the team bus at an away game.

But the corn crib was sacred, an understood and unspoken out-of-bounds area.

Until now.

Shawn Cooper leaped up as I started to put the bus in gear.

"Are we going to stand for this?" he shouted. "Are we going to let them get away with this?"

The rush of noise was frightening. Even the little kids in front were caught up in the anger, jumping up out of their seats, shouting along with the older ones.

I tried to block the aisle, but just as fast, they had the back door open and began jumping out as the warning buzzer screamed in my ear. The kids just behind me slipped by, and as I tried to block the door again, they pushed and shoved their way down the steps. My heart was in my throat as I followed.

Everyone came to a halt at the front fender. The Spring Hill kids with the paintbrushes reminded me of deer caught in a spotlight, on their toes, ready to run, eyes wide and frightened.

Shawn stood at the head of the group, looking for all the world like a blond pit bull with his hackles up. I knew it would take only a wrong word, a mistaken motion, to set off a full-scale fight. I shoved my way through my bus charges and pretended I had control of the situation.

"Everyone who's not on that bus in sixty seconds will spend the rest of his or her life in detention hall," I said. The little kids scattered for the bus, all but Matt Leonard, a first-grader. He tugged on my sweater.

"Mrs. Gulley?" he said.

I didn't take my eyes off the high-school kids who had made no attempt to get back to the bus.

"Matt, get on the bus," I spoke sharply. Then to the high-schoolers, "You've got fifteen seconds."

Understanding

Shawn shook his head. "We can't let this happen," he breathed, his fists clenched. The five boys and two girls behind him murmured assent.

One of the kids in the cornfield spoke for the first time. "This isn't what it looks like, man," he called.

Shawn's short laugh sent chills down my spine. "Of course it's not," he yelled back. "You got caught." And he called the Spring Hill boy a name that made even the girls wince.

"Mrs. Gulley?" The little hand tugging again.

I pushed it away. The air was charged with electricity. "OK," I whispered, standing nose to nose with Shawn. "Here's the deal. We get out of here right now or I'll have the superintendent, the principal, and the county sheriff here in five minutes."

The hand was pulling on my clothes again. "Mrs. Gulley . . ."

I whirled and almost shouted, "What is it, Matt?"

Matt's big blue eyes filled with quick tears at the tone of my voice. "Mrs. Gulley," he gulped, "I don't think they painted the bad words. I think they're painting over them!"

We all turned to stare at the old, rickety building, and with a rush like air out of a burst balloon, I felt the tension whoosh away.

It was true. The graffiti was scribbled in reds and whites and blacks . . . now the whole end of the building was a bright blue, the color of the sky.

The color dripping from the trembling paint brushes.

Shawn unclenched his fists and rubbed his hands together nervously, clearing his throat. The seven behind him were staring at the ground, the clouds in the sky, the bus behind them . . . anything but the Spring Hill group in the field.

"So . . . what's the deal?" Shawn finally blurted.

"We don't know for sure," the other kid said. "Coulda been us. We don't know. But we did know you'd blame us. So . . ." He gestured toward the building with his brush and shrugged. "We're not all bad," he added.

After a moment, one of the boys behind Shawn stepped forward, shoved him playfully, and walked into the field. He picked up a discarded brush and grinned, lifting his eyebrows. The rest followed, Shawn last.

Exasperated, I watched them all smearing sky-blue paint on the old building, wondering how in the world I was going to explain this when I came in so late.

Then, just as quickly, I decided it really didn't matter. Sometimes life's best lessons are learned nowhere near a classroom.

Section 3

Christmas Wishes

THE LEAST ONES

I'd been told about the new kid who'd moved into the old Carson rental house, and as I braked my school bus to a stop at the end of his driveway, I could see the warning was right on target.

Conner Lewis was short and square and looked much older than the other second-graders on my bus. He'd been held back a grade, but still, there was entirely too much bitterness etched into the grimy lines on his cheeks and forehead, too much adult knowledge in his dark eyes. I took a deep breath as I pulled the bifold door open and pasted on what I hoped passed for a smile.

"Hi, Conner," I said. "Welcome to bus number nine."

He looked at me for a second, then walked up the steps. His heavy dark brows narrowed. He glanced from kid to kid, as though committing each face to memory. They stared back with looks ranging from amusement to loathing. Most of them had already heard about Conner.

The second-grader was a BD kid—behavioral disorder. He would attend Mrs. Larson's special BD class each morning.

Within thirty seconds, I was wondering if I'd be able to get him to school at all. He walked right past me, heading for the seats in the back of the bus.

"Hey, Conner," I called. "All the grade-school kids sit up here."

"Why?" He stood where he was.

"Because I said so," I told him.

The Least Ones

"I want to sit here." He plunked down into the last seat.

I started to unbutton my seat belt. "Conner, please come back here."

"No," he said, his voice getting louder. The rest of the kids were silent, waiting to see how this power struggle would end.

I started down the bus aisle and watched Conner hurl himself into a first-class tantrum. He started to scream.

"I'm not sitting up there! You can't make me! I want to sit here!"

I took hold of his collar and pulled him to his feet. I was likely to get in big trouble for physically touching him, but at that moment, I just didn't care. He swung his fists furiously at me.

"Let me go!" he shrieked. "I'll kill you! I don't want to sit up there."

I tightened my grip until he followed me to where I wanted him. Then I let him go. He plunked into the seat, his lower lip sticking out in a big baby pout.

"This is a stupid bus," he cried. "*You're* stupid. I want to go back to my old school. I don't want to ride this bus." He went on and on until my head was pounding. But he stayed in the seat as I put the bus in gear and started down the road.

By the time we pulled into the grade-school parking lot, my headache was full blown. I had told Conner to "be quiet and sit down" so many times, I felt like a broken record. He jumped up and down and every other direction in his seat, trying to annoy anyone within reach. I swung the door open and thought briefly about throwing him out, but I was in enough trouble already.

The rest of the grade-schoolers bounced down the steps like brightly colored jumping beans. All but Conner.

"Where do I go?" he asked.

"Don't you know what room you're in? What's your teacher's name?"

He looked at me blankly.

"Didn't your mom bring you to school to register?"

He shook his head. "Mom just said to go to school."

It was hard to believe a mom would just shove her kid onto the bus and send him off to school on the first day, but I took his grimy hand and led him to the office. The secretary took one look and smiled sadly.

"God, I hate to see one of these," she whispered. "I'll give him a month here. Then she'll drag him somewhere else. Poor little kid doesn't have a chance."

I was ashamed as I watched her take his hand and lead him down the hall to his second-grade room. His ragged pants were inches too short; his shirt lacked buttons, the sleeves ending just short of his wrists. His life was tough enough. Maybe I could be more patient with him.

It wasn't easy. Conner continued to be loud and obnoxious and often vulgar. The other kids treated him in a like manner.

"How many years has it been since you took a shower, Conner?"

"Do you think you might comb your hair this month, Conner?"

"Don't you have any other clothes, Conner?"

Conner loved every word. Attention was attention. The more they teased, the more he asked for it. The situation was spiraling out of my control, and I knew it had to stop. Easier said than done, but I had an idea.

"Conner, I have a job for you," I told him one morning. The little boy frowned. He wasn't much into following directions.

"Since you're sitting in the front seat anyway, how about being my door opener?"

Now I had his attention. This was a position of power. Happily, he pulled the door open at each stop, shutting it securely behind each rider.

From then on, the problems eased. Conner was so intent on being a perfect "door man" that he had little time to cause trouble. The other kids were forced to accept him as a member of the group through sheer jealousy.

His dirty face and devilish grin were starting to tug at my heart. I was surprised to find myself actually smiling when I caught sight of the little figure standing by the mailbox. Sometimes he looked so bad, I took him to the teacher's lounge and scrubbed his face and combed his hair. I couldn't understand why a mom would send her kid to school that way.

The Least Ones

I'd learned a little about her. It was rumored that she seemed to have a lot of men friends. I'd seen for myself the strange cars in the driveway. Conner stared at them resentfully when he got off the bus, the only time he was quiet. He'd seem so small and vulnerable as he walked toward the house.

Soon, Christmas break was just a few weeks away. Each year, I gave little gifts to my bus kids—a candy bar or candy cane—but this holiday season I wanted to give one that would be special.

It was going to be a challenge. I'd already tried to give Conner a warm coat I'd found at a yard sale. Even on the coldest days, he wore a ragged sweatshirt that barely covered his arms. The next morning he gave the coat back.

"Mom says we don't take no charity," he said, but his eyes betrayed how much it hurt him.

I looked up the hill and saw she was standing just inside the screen door, a shadow, smoke drifting out from the cigarette she held.

What could I give him that would be acceptable? Finally I bought a yellow school bus with real rubber tires that turned. I painted the bus number on the fender and wrote "Conner's Door," on the bifold door. It was perfect. I knew he'd love it.

The next morning, the last day of school before vacation, I pulled to a stop in front of Conner's house, all the red and yellow flashers blinking merrily like Christmas lights. No little figure stood by the mailbox. There was silence on the bus as we all looked up the hill, waiting. I could hear the screen door squeak as it swung aimlessly in the wind. A tattered curtain fluttered out an open window. I took a deep breath, then another.

And then I had to face what I'd known in my heart all along. There was so little I could do to help all the little Conners in the world. I clutched the tiny toy school bus helplessly in my hand and stared at the cold, empty house.

Conner's mother had moved on.

A LITTLE HELP TO FIND THE WAY

It was the Friday before Christmas and the last day of school. The snow was bright, the sky crystal clear as I headed out into the country to drop my bus kids off for the final time before Christmas vacation. I could almost hear the sound of sleigh bells. But as I steered my school bus carefully down the snow-covered country roads, I wasn't anticipating the Christmas season with the joy and hope I'd always had in the past. I glanced up in my overhead rearview mirror at the kids behind me. They were talking and giggling much more than usual, excited about what Christmas would bring.

But I knew most weren't looking forward to the celebration of the birth of the Christ Child, not even the special caring and sharing feelings that flow with the season. They were only concerned about what was going to be under the Christmas tree, what Santa was going to bring, the brightly wrapped packages Mom and Dad would sneak into the house when they thought no one was looking.

Kids had changed. Their ideas about the Christmas season had changed. Some of the kids on my bus knew no other reason for December 25th than Santa. My heart was sick as I looked at the young faces reflected in my mirror. They were good kids, most of them, but somehow, the true—the only—reason for Christmas had gotten away from them.

I was still lost in thought when I caught sight of the woman standing on the shoulder of the gravel road. Her car was turned at a steep angle almost into the ditch. She waved a gloved hand at me, and as I slowed to a stop and put the emergency flashers on, I thought she might have had an accident. In a way, it turned out to be worse.

"Hello," the elderly woman called, smiling brightly. At first glance, she appeared to be neatly dressed in a polyester skirt and jacket, but as I stepped off the bus, I saw that her blue checkered jacket was buttoned up one button off. Her white hair floated a little wildly around her face. Alarm bells went off in my mind.

"Are you OK?" I asked.

She smiled at me. "Oh, sure," she replied cheerfully. "It's just that I need to buy some Christmas presents for my grandchildren, and I can't seem to find the mall."

It took my breath away. She was miles out in the country, far from any shopping mall.

"I was driving around, and I saw the bus coming, so I thought I'd stop you and ask. I'm Loretta Thomas," she said, almost as an afterthought, as though she hoped I knew who she was.

"You've been driving around to find the mall?" I asked.

"No," she said, still cheerful. "I'm trying to find my house. I've been driving in circles for a long time."

Circles. And now I knew for sure what was going on. Finding the mall was no longer the problem. I asked her where she lived, and she named a city street I'd never heard of.

"Is it near here?" I asked. I wanted to ask, "Do you know where you are right now?" But I didn't.

"I think it is," she said. "I don't know." Her smile faded just the least little bit, and she looked frightened and unsure of herself.

"What's it near?" I asked. "Any big streets?"

Then I forced myself to stop talking to her as if she were a five-year-old who had wandered away from home.

But she was, almost. And the results were the same.

By now, several of the older kids from the bus were at the door, listening. Amber Pearson, a senior girl whose big problem all week had been what to wear for her weekend date, pulled a cell phone out of her pocket. "I'll call my mom," she said. "Maybe she knows where that street is." She dialed, and I saw her glance at Loretta as she talked.

I turned to look at the kids in the bus doorway, and I knew most of them had it figured out. Amber's friend, Dawn Garcia, stood next to the elderly woman, making small talk. "Hi. I'm Dawn," she said, putting a comforting hand on the woman's arm. "Do you have any kids?" she asked.

The woman's face brightened. "My daughter and her family are up north," she said. "I have a son, too. I can't think where he lives." She frowned, her eyes glancing here and there with the frightened look again.

"How many grandchildren do you have?" Dawn asked quickly.

Loretta's brow creased as she frowned again in thought. "Six, I think. Yes, six." Her smile was back. "Madison, Jeremy, Tyler . . . ah . . . Jared . . . ah . . . " Her voice trailed off. "I'll think of their names in a bit," she said, more to reassure herself than Dawn, it seemed.

"That's a lot of Christmas presents," Dawn said. "I'll bet you could use some help shopping. Maybe my friend, Amber, and I could pick you up this weekend and take you to the mall."

The woman's eyes brightened, then filled with tears. "Oh, would you, dear? That would be so wonderful. I seem . . . I seem to have a little trouble finding the store."

Sam Hixson, who was only eight, tugged at her sleeve. "We can help you make a list," he said, "while we're waiting." Other little kids gathered around us, asking the age of the woman's grandkids, making suggestions, arguing over who would like what.

"Your granddaughter, Madison, is nine?" Kendra Lawson asked. "I'm nine, too. I bet I know what she wants for Christmas."

Sam carefully printed all the suggestions on a big sheet of school paper.

By the time Amber's mom arrived, a complete Christmas list and arrangements to go shopping had been made. As Mrs. Pearson stepped out of her car, she looked at the elderly woman standing next to the bus. Without anyone saying a word, she seemed to understand the problem. Reaching into the side pocket on the door, she brought out a big map and unfolded it on the hood of her car. We looked at it carefully, searching for the street name Loretta had given us. We couldn't find it.

"Are you sure that's the right street?" Dawn asked ever so gently.

A Little Help to Find the Way

"Yes, I'm sure of it," the elderly woman said. "I've lived there . . . well, forever."

OK. We searched again, all of us hovering around the map, and finally Amber pointed one long, lacquered fingernail at a tiny street in the city. "Here it is," she cried.

And it was. Now how to get Loretta home? Amber had the answer. Her mom could drive the woman's car, and Amber, who had her driver's license, could follow in the Pearson's car.

As they drove away, everyone waved and shouted Goodbye. We watched the two cars disappear in the distance, and then the kids took their seats to continue the ride home.

The bus was quiet now. I looked back at the young faces and thought about how wrong I'd been. Somehow, without being told, these kids had found the spirit of Christmas in their hearts. These least ones had, all on their own, offered the very heart of the Christmas season to an old, confused woman who'd lost her way.

They stared silently out the window, and I knew each of them had put aside what Santa was going to bring them. I knew they were thinking about an elderly lady driving in circles, trying to find her way home.

FRIENDSHIP IS EVERYTHING

The sun sparkled like diamonds on the new snow lining the narrow country road as I steered my school bus between the knee-high drifts. The sky was brilliant blue with cold. Any other day, I would have been cheered by the beauty of the December day. But this morning, I relived the night two weeks ago over and over in my mind. My dad's still form on the living-room floor, the wail of a siren in the distance. He was dying. I knew it. I could see the life fading from his face.

"Dad," I'd whispered. "Hold on. The paramedics are coming."

I held his hand and watched him take his last breath, and there was nothing I could do to stop it. I couldn't stop it.

That was the hardest part.

My sister had tried to comfort me. I knew what she had said was true. He'd been so ill and had suffered so much the past few years. It was better this way. And yet I ached with the anguish of being helpless. I couldn't stop the dying. And I couldn't stop the nightmare in my mind or the pain in my heart.

The kids behind me were quiet—unusual this close to Christmas. They avoided my eyes. It's the way children deal with death. A few told me they were sorry to hear about my dad. But I knew they didn't really understand. Kids don't have much of a concept of mortality. Dying, to them, is something that happens to other people—old people—and never to them. It was the last day of school before

Friendship Is Everything

Christmas vacation, and I knew by the time school started again, they would have forgotten all about my dad.

I watched them bounce down the steps at each stop, excited about two weeks of vacation and the presents and fun that were to be. I wondered how we'd get through Christmas, my sister, my mom, and I. A family time. Watching the fantasy families on TV, hearing the songs and carols, listening for my dad's voice. The hurt, the guilt I felt pressed like a boulder upon my chest until I could barely breathe.

Later that afternoon, as I sat in a chair mindlessly watching a Christmas show, a knock on the door brought me out of the same old nightmares. My three best friends stood there.

"We're going out," Jan said. She and Jean took my arms, giving me no chance to argue. Dutch grabbed my coat out of the front closet, and off we went. We sped through the mall, buying little gifts for my mom, my sister and her family, and anyone else my friends could think of. Then they took me to my favorite restaurant and ordered what they knew I liked best.

"Do you know how many years we've all been friends?" Jan asked. We all knew. Almost all our lives.

"We've helped each other through marriages, births, divorces, and death," Dutch told me. She put her hand over mine. "And we're all going to get through this," she said.

I told them about the nightmares, the helplessness, the guilt clutching my very soul because I couldn't keep my own dad from dying.

Not one tried to tell me I was being silly or foolish, that there had been nothing, after all, that I could do. Or should have done.

Jan smiled as she listened. "I think it's from Ecclesiastes," she said, quoting, " 'To everything there is a season, a time for every purpose under heaven.' "

Dutch nodded. "It was time," she said. "Your dad was ready. And you know what? You won't feel this way forever. When a little time has passed, the pain will ease, and you'll be filled instead with wonderful memories. Cherish them all."

It was a wonderful evening. When I went home that night and called my mom, I found each of my friends had also called her, "just to talk," she said. Her voice sounded brighter.

We made it through that first Christmas without Dad. After the holidays, either Jan, Dutch, or Jean—sometimes all three—showed up on my doorstep to "do lunch" or go shopping or simply to be with me. Several times, they picked up my mom, and we all went out together. And as the days went on, I found they were right; the keen cutting edges of guilt softened.

When I started out on my school bus route the Monday morning after vacation, the day was overcast and gray, but my world was less dark.

Madison, a third-grader, was my very first stop. She looked up at me uncertainly, suddenly remembering my loss. I smiled, and she smiled back, relieved.

"What did your friends get you for Christmas, Mrs. Gulley?" she asked.

My heart felt lighter as I answered. "Their love and friendship," I said.

Madison frowned, "Is that all?" she asked, disappointed.

"Oh, Madison," I said, hugging her close, hoping someday she'd understand. "That's everything."

THE BEST GIFT

The thin, scraggly little girl smiled brightly as I braked the school bus to a stop next to her driveway. Her heavy blond hair framed a tiny, pale face with eyes so dark they reminded me of black buttons on a snowman. Even though the temperature was barely above freezing, she wore only white summer sandals and a sleeveless cotton dress, covered with a long, white, ragged-looking sweater that I knew had to be her mother's. She was shivering on this bitter December day, the last week before Christmas vacation, but she hopped up the steps into the bus with the optimism of a six-year-old. In her bare hands, her fingers white with cold, she held a small box wrapped in homemade Christmas paper.

"Good morning, Mrs. Gulley," she said. "I have a Christmas present for you." She held the gift out to me, her eyes shining with pride and hope. I placed it on the small stack of gifts next to me, my heart aching with uncertainty.

"Thank you, Sandy," I replied, looking at her tattered sweater and bare red toes. I turned the heater switch up to high, hoping some of the warmth would make its way to the grade-school seats.

Some of the families in our small school district were living on less than adequate incomes, but none were as out-and-out poor as the Hintons. A single mother, Marie Hinton did the best she could for her two small daughters, three-year-old Chris, and Sandy, who was a first-grader, but without an education or work skills and no support from an absent husband, her best barely avoided starvation.

I didn't have a clue how Sandy's poor clothes kept her from freezing, but at least she ate breakfast and lunch at school. I hated to think about how Marie and Chris managed.

Now, just before Christmas, I had another worry. I always passed out little Christmas gifts to my bus kids, and most of them gave me small presents in return, usually picked out and purchased by Mom or Dad. They'd been excited about the gift exchange for weeks, whispering and giggling.

"Mrs. Gulley, what do you want for Christmas?" one of the first-graders had asked me weeks ago.

"Oh, I really don't need presents this year," I told them, watching Sandy in the overhead mirror. "Just having you on my bus is present enough."

They all laughed. No one took it seriously. They went ahead with their plans, each one trying to outdo the other and give me the "best gift."

Sandy had watched and listened. I'd seen the look on her face, and I agonized for her.

This morning, each child had handed me a gift of some sort, almost all neatly wrapped in store-bought paper, decorated with bright bows. All but Sandy's. I looked at the lined school paper adorned with the six-year-old's crayon drawings of trees and ornaments.

If only I could figure out a way to delay the gift opening, maybe take everything home for a private unwrapping. But the kids had always insisted I do it before they went into school. Today was no different. They were all on their feet almost as soon as we pulled up to the grade school and braked to a stop.

"Open your presents, Mrs. Gulley," they started to shout. "We want to see."

It was tradition, and it was expected. And always before it had been so much fun. Now I was afraid.

Finally, while my bus riders watched with excitement, I began to open the brightly wrapped boxes and envelopes one by one. I tried to gasp and exclaim over each box of chocolate-covered cherries, tree ornament, or head scarf as though it were the one and only thing I'd wanted all my life.

The Best Gift

Finally, I reached for Sandy's gift. The others whispered and waited. With great care, I pulled the homemade wrapping off and removed the lid of the small box.

The box was empty. I looked at her, puzzled. She wasn't at all embarrassed. Her face was filled with pride and hope.

"It's empty," I whispered. I didn't know what to do.

The other kids who could see started to laugh. "There's nothing in it," another first-grader hooted. "Sandy gave Mrs. Gulley an empty box." There were out-and-out shrieks of laughter.

Sandy shrank back into the seat, her smile fading. Tears began to glisten in the corners of her eyes. She shook her head, the mane of blond hair swinging about her shoulders and across her face.

"No," she whispered back. "It's full. I blew one hundred Christmas kisses into it for you."

The world stood still, and for a moment I was unaware of anything else around us.

Sandy saw the instant tears in my eyes and thought she'd done something wrong. Her uncertain smile crumpled completely.

"Don't you like it?" she asked.

Like it? I thought. Of all the kids on my bus who had the resources to give me anything and everything, this least one had managed to give the spirit, the very heart, of the season. I gathered her into my arms, my only defense against blubbering in front of the other kids.

"It's my very favorite," I said, hugging her close. "How did you know homemade gifts are my very favorite?"

A LOVE STORY

My hands were welded to the steering wheel of my school bus as though our lives depended on it, but it wasn't because of the snow-covered roads. All morning I'd been listening to the kids on my school bus talk about marriage. Trashing the whole idea would be a better statement. The whole conversation had started because Grace Sheller's mom and dad were getting a divorce. She was only eight, and I'd seen the tears each morning long before she made the big announcement to her friends.

"My daddy's going to move away," she'd cried. "I'll only see him once a month."

The other little kids were sympathetic. "My mommy lives a long way away," offered Tyler Moore, a third-grader. "But she calls me, and she comes to get me every Saturday."

Monty Delf wasn't so positive. "Yeah, well, my dad doesn't have time for me," he grumbled. "He says his new job is too busy, but he went to Jamaica with his girlfriend last week." Monty was thirteen, and life had been tough for him since his parents had divorced.

"I'm never getting married." It was Cheyenne Lang, one of the most popular girls in the high school. "It's not worth it. You can just live with someone. Then, if it doesn't work out, all you have to do is leave."

My heart ached as I listened to them talk. I didn't know what to say. At least half the kids on my bus came from divorced families.

A Love Story

And heaven only knew what they heard and saw before the parents went their separate ways.

A *sign of the times*, I thought. A horrible sign of where the world was headed. It seemed to be spreading everywhere—apathy toward the most important things in life. There seemed to be no loyalty or enthusiasm in the workplace from employees, no strong responsibilities to each other within the family unit, and the attitude seemed especially true for a husband and wife. Celebrities changed mates like shoes. What role models could these little ones look up to? How could they learn anything about love and caring and commitment when the world around them was teaching by example that none of it mattered?

I was so upset I almost didn't see the car just around the corner at the crossroad. The older sedan was tilted into the ditch, the passenger side wheels buried in deep snow, and a man was trying to shovel it free. I braked to a stop, backed up to the crossroad, and opened the door.

"Can I get help for you?" I called. The man looked up, and I could see he was very old. He dropped the shovel and trudged wearily to the bus.

"Would you mind if I warmed up a bit?" He asked. "I think I can get it out, but my hands are so cold."

"Of course," I said. "Come in and sit down." I radioed my boss that I might be a few minutes late. When the elderly man slid into a front seat and removed his jacket hood, I saw that he was even older than I'd thought. His hair was white and thin, his skin wrinkled and red from the cold. But his eyes were dark and bright, twinkling with life.

"I'm Jack," he said. "Jackson Stuart. My kids went to school here years ago, but in nothing so fancy as this bus." His grin made his leathery, lined face light up.

He pulled his gloves off, and one of the little kids behind him cried out. "You're bleeding," Todd said. "You hurt yourself."

"Oh," Jack said, examining his hand. "So I have. When you get old, your skin is so thin." He smiled down at the first-grader.

"Why don't I just call a tow truck for you?" I asked. "It's too cold out there for you to try to shovel it out by yourself."

He shook his head. "I don't have time," he said. "It'd take a long while for them to get out here on a day like this. I'd be way down on the list. I think I can do it myself. I have an important date at nine."

I took down the first-aid kit and pulled out a bandage. As I wrapped it around his finger, we talked, and I asked where he had to be at nine. I chuckled to myself thinking about this old man and his "date."

"I have to be at the nursing home to have breakfast with my wife," he said. "I go every morning for breakfast with her. I talk to her about when we met and all the good times we've had. In fact, today I was going to remind her about the time we got stuck in the snow and spent all morning waiting for the tow truck." His smile trembled, as a faraway look clouded his eyes. "We had to cuddle close to keep warm."

"Will she be worried if you're late?" I asked, finishing with the bandage. "My boss can call her from the school-bus garage."

The old man smiled gently. "I don't think that'll work," he said. "She has Alzheimer's disease. She doesn't even know who I am." His eyes brightened with tears as he added, "She hasn't recognized me for five years now."

The bus began to quiet down as the kids listened.

"And you're still going every morning even though she doesn't know who you are?" I asked.

He smiled again and patted my hand. It was as though he felt sorry for me because I didn't understand.

"She doesn't know me," he said, "but I still know who she is. And even more important, I remember who she *was.*"

The bus was silent now. Every kid had heard.

"But don't you feel bad that she won't ever know you again?" It was Cody Williams, the second-grader sitting beside Jack.

The man looked at Cody. "Of course I do," he said. "But love— really true love—is an acceptance of all that is." He looked up into my overhead rearview mirror, and his eyes seemed to travel from child to child. "It's acceptance of all that has been, will be, and . . ." he hesitated, and I saw the sorrow on his face, ". . . and all that will not be," he finished.

I had to swallow hard to keep the tears from spilling out of my overfull eyes. Just then I heard some throats clear, and three of the

A Love Story

biggest guys from the football squad saved me from blubbering in front of everyone. I felt the bus rock as they walked to the front.

"Mrs. Gulley?" they said. "How about if we dig the car out. It won't take us five minutes."

I hesitated. Then I looked again at how red the old man's face was. I nodded. "OK," I told them.

When they'd moved enough snow to free the car, they waved for Jack to get into the driver's seat so they could push him back on the road. He nodded his thanks to me and went out into the cold. I saw him wave as he drove away to keep his "date."

As I put the bus in gear and we moved down the road, there wasn't a sound. I hoped the silence meant each of the children behind me was re-evaluating his or her idea of love and commitment and how things should be in the world.

God had sent them a pretty good role model.

Section 4

Country Roads

WHEN IT COUNTS

I heard the crunch from the rear of the bus and knew instantly what it was. I put on the brake, turned off the key, and rested my head on the steering wheel.

I had just backed over Jed Larson's mailbox.

The noise from the engine hadn't faded before the door on the ancient, peeling, two-story farmhouse slammed open.

"Uh-oh," a high-schooler in the back seat said. "You're in trouble now, Mrs. Gulley."

A thin, white-haired man in patched jeans trundled toward the bus, waving one bony fist in the air. His mouth was moving, but he was, as yet, too far away for his shouts to be heard. How I wished it could have remained that way! This year alone he'd called the bus garage to complain—once about me raising too much dust, once because a kid had tossed a paper out a window into his yard, and three times because I'd come too close to his flower garden while backing out of the Kincaids' driveway across the road.

In addition, he stopped me once or twice a week to complain personally about something—anything, everything. I tried my best to be patient and to be as careful as I could, but now with the road piled high with snowdrifts, it was hard to maneuver in the narrow road and driveway. There wasn't a prayer that Mr. Larson would accept that as an excuse for a smashed mailbox, but it was all I had.

When It Counts

I watched him grumble his way down the driveway and wearily climbed out of the bus to meet him.

"Don't they make you go to school to learn to drive that cockeyed piece of machinery?" The elderly man's voice was thin and filled with anger. "As if the ruts in the road aren't bad enough, you have to run over my cockeyed mailbox."

I took a deep breath. "I'm sorry, Mr. Larson. I just couldn't get it cranked hard enough with that drift in the Kincaids' drive. The district will replace it for you."

The wind was blowing like crazy, and I shivered with the cold. Jed Larson didn't even have a coat on, but I was pretty sure the red flush of rage coloring his craggy neck and face was keeping him warm enough.

"Oh, the district will replace it, will they? And will they deliver my mail to the door today? I'm sure as blazes not going to stand out here in the snow and wait for it!"

He went on and on, and I tried to smile and nod, wondering what made an old man so cranky and obnoxious, finally deciding this one had been born that way. At last I backed to the bus, bolted up the steps, and turned the key, still hearing his shrill voice through the closed door as we drove away. The phone would be ringing off the wall at the bus garage in the time it took Mr. Larson to get back to his house.

By the time I delivered the last of the kids to school, the wind had grown to a full-blown roar and the roads were starting to drift. As I headed back to the bus garage, I had a bad feeling in the pit of my stomach that had nothing to do with Jed Larson's mailbox.

I pulled the bus into line and parked it. As I gathered up my things to leave, my supervisor appeared at the bus door, his face red with cold, brow crinkled with worry.

"There's an unexpected storm coming through," he shouted over the wind and snow pelting the bus. "It's supposed to be nasty. School's just been canceled. We're heading right back to take the kids home."

Even as I roared out of the last school and back into the country with fifty kids, a tiny, remote part of my heart told me it was wrong. They were thrilled with the excitement of getting a day off, chattering happily, giggling, doing kid things. Only a few of the older kids were staring out the window into the storm, their eyes troubled.

The road in front of the bus had disappeared, everything white. If I hadn't traveled this way a thousand times before, I wouldn't have had a clue where we were. As it was, I almost felt my way to my first stop. Kids ran down the steps through the opened door and scattered into the white nothingness. I took a deep breath, put the bus in gear, and moved forward.

Out of the white wall, a monster lumbered toward me, eyes blinking red and yellow. Behind me a little girl shrieked, and I clamped my jaw shut to keep from doing the same thing. The creature stopped, and I recognized it as a huge, tandem-wheel farm tractor. A man climbed down and fought his way through the snow to the bus door. There was something familiar about him, but I was stunned when he pulled the hood off his parka.

"Mr. Larson," I stammered.

"You'll never make it down this road alone," he shouted, the wind whipping his hair, making him look like a madman. "Follow the tractor. I'll break the drifts and lead you through it."

I was too speechless to do more than nod. He climbed back on the tractor, and we moved forward, but this time I felt safe as I followed the flashing lights. When we had delivered the last rider home, the old farmer guided me to the edge of town, where we were sheltered somewhat from the fierce wind.

I pulled over, and Mr. Larson climbed aboard the bus again, pulling off his gloves to warm his hands next to the heater.

I finally got the courage to whisper, "Thank you."

He nodded, and took a deep breath. "Had some kids of my own once," he said, staring into the wind and snow. "They were killed in a car wreck. The wife, she never got over it. Died with the hurt still in her heart, I guess."

He wiped his eyes, rubbed his temples, smoothed at the white hair. "Awful hard to see those kids go by every day," he whispered so low I could barely hear. "Awful hard."

He looked at me then and nodded again. Then he walked down the steps and into the storm.

PLAYING WITH FIRE

Even though they seldom think so, teenage girls are beautiful, if nothing else just by being young and hopeful. And I always liked to think most of the high-school girls on my bus had brains as well as good looks.

It seemed as though Vonna Lestor was always going out of her way to prove me wrong. About the brains, that is. She was pretty enough, tall, thin, and long-waisted with a woman's figure. She had dark hair that usually flowed in heavy waves down her back but sometimes was pulled up on top of her head in glossy ringlets. Sometimes when she walked onto the bus, wearing her standard uniform of a tight sweater and jeans, I didn't know whether to laugh or yell at her.

She draped herself over every boy who held still long enough . . . which was most of them. I was amazed that none of them saw through her phony exterior, and even more surprised that Bryan Bilaggi chose to go steady with her. I liked Bryan. He'd ridden my bus since kindergarten, and just the fact that he chose to go with Vonna made me think there had to be some good in her that I was missing. Bryan was an all-right kid.

But the day Vonna stomped up the bus steps and threw herself into her seat, arms crossed with anger, I had no idea what a self-centered troll she truly was and how what she was going to do would change all of our lives forever.

"What a jerk!" I heard her complain to Bryan, sitting next to her. "I didn't have that stupid report done, and he gave me another stupid detention. I hate him!"

"Vonna," I said, "quiet down."

When I glanced up in the overhead mirror, I saw her stick her tongue out at me. Then she turned around and faced the back, her shoulders set in a stiff and furious line.

For the rest of the trip home, I heard enough of the conversation to know she was talking about her science teacher, Charles Swift. She complained regularly about her teachers, but she'd settled on Charlie with a viciousness that took my breath away.

Charlie had taught in our small school system for years. He was the type of guy everyone liked—even the kids—although he ran his classes with a no-nonsense attitude. He demanded the best from the kids he taught and accepted no less. I knew Vonna pretty much depended on charming her way through most of her classes, but Charlie would have none of it. He made it plain that she actually had to work in his class to earn her grade.

"She thinks her looks will get her anywhere she wants to go in life," he'd told me once. "Doesn't have a clue, that one." He shook his head, a wry smile creasing his leathery face.

"Life's going to be hard for her."

I was surprised to hear him say that. I couldn't imagine how life could be hard for a kid who seemed to have it all.

Now I watched in my overhead mirror as Bryan tried to talk sense into Vonna, teasing her, trying to cheer her up.

"Hey, it's OK," I heard him say. "I'll help you with the report. I'll wait after detention hall and find us a ride home."

"That's not the point," Vonna whined. "He's picking on me. He does it all the time. I hate his guts."

Then I saw her eyes narrow, and I could barely hear the next words. "He's not going to get away with it this time," she said, her voice hissing like a snake. "He's going to be sorry. I'm going to make sure he's the sorriest man alive."

The look on her face made a chill run up my back. All weekend, I thought about what she'd said. It worried me. Monday morning I found out why.

Playing With Fire

There was a message waiting for me after my bus run, asking me to come to the high-school principal's office immediately. It was an unusual request, and I walked into the school with some misgivings. Amy Fisher, the high-school girls' physical education teacher, was just leaving the office. "I think you should know," she whispered, "Vonna and her parents have filed serious charges against Charlie."

What was she talking about? "Charges?" I repeated.

"Yep," she said, "the kid says he 'touched her inappropriately.' "

"What a crock," I said indignantly. "Charlie would never do a thing like that. She's just trying to get even because he won't take any of her . . ."

"I know," Amy sighed. "But the authorities have to check it out. You know how that goes these days. We'll just have to stand behind Charlie."

"Well, I think I can do better than that," I said. I marched into Principal Anderson's office. I told him in detail what Vonna had said on the bus the week before and gave him the names of the girls Vonna had been talking to.

"I've known Charlie for fifteen years," I finished. "Even if I hadn't heard what Vonna said, I'd still swear he'd never do what she is accusing him of."

Principal Anderson took a deep breath and nodded. "We were sure that was the case," he said, "but we had nothing but Charlie's word against hers. I think we can get to the bottom of this, if you'd be willing to repeat your story to the authorities."

The rest of the week was a nightmare of police investigators and counselors, as well as students and teachers whispering in the halls. By midweek, the word was out. Vonna had admitted to the authorities that she'd lied. Friday, I went in to talk to Charlie, relieved that the charges had been dropped and everything had been straightened out. I was surprised to see him pulling things out of his desk drawers, placing them into a cardboard box on the desk.

"What's up?" I asked, a stone settling onto my chest.

He turned around and smiled at me. A big man with gentle eyes, his face framed by a mop of brown hair peppered with gray, he reminded me of a kindly bear. "Just packing up," he said, looking away. "Just packing up."

I sat down in a student desk. "But why?" I whispered. Teaching was his life.

"These past few years I've often thought about retiring," he said without looking up. "I think this is the time."

"But it's OK," I insisted. "She admitted she lied."

He paused for a moment, looking out the window at something I couldn't see.

"I've been accused of fire," he said finally. "And I've been found not guilty. But . . ."

He turned to look at me, and I knew what he was going to say. "How many mothers are going to worry about their daughters walking into my class," he said. It was not a question. "How many people are going to stand around in the post office or the library or the local café and talk about whether or not I can be trusted to be in the same room with little girls?"

A sick feeling settled into the pit of my stomach as I realized the truth in what he said. "You're too tough to let that scare you," I whispered.

He smiled and shook his head. Then turned back to his packing. "The smoke remains," he said softly.

I had no answer for him. I knew it was true. He picked up the box, a lifetime of teaching, and walked out of the room. I heard the click of his heels echoing down the empty hall.

That afternoon I saw Vonna walking from the high school toward the bus, and I had to fold my hands tightly together as she came up the steps and stood next to me, facing the other kids. A self-satisfied smirk spread across her face. I wondered how I had ever thought she was pretty. Never had I wanted to hurt a person as badly as I wanted to hurt her. But something inside me told me to wait.

"Well?" she said, grinning. "Did I do it or what? I got rid of the jerk."

There was some rustling around in the high-school seats. A coldness was settling into the bus that even Vonna was beginning to feel. Her smile faltered just a little.

Playing With Fire

"So . . ." Ashley Stiles said, "you lied." Again, it wasn't a question.

The bus was so quiet now, I could hear Vonna's breathing beside me. Quickly, she slid into the seat next to Bryan, her smile gone, her face uncertain.

And then I was glad I hadn't said anything to her. I was beginning to understand what Charlie meant when he said life was going to be hard for Vonna. I took a deep breath and relaxed my hands, waiting for what I was sure was going to happen next.

Bryan gathered his books together and stood up. He looked down at Vonna. "I liked Mr. Swift," he said. Without another word, he moved to another seat.

As I headed the bus out of the parking lot and into the country, I glanced in my overhead mirror. Vonna was frozen in her seat, motionless and alone. I told myself this was just a teenage girl with bad judgment, a child who was about to learn a hard lesson. I should have felt a twinge of pity for her.

But God help me, I was glad.

WHAT WILL BE

The crudely drawn cardboard sign pointed down a gravel road west of my school bus route. "Free puppies," it read. I took note and decided I would investigate. My sister-in-law had just been forced to put down her elderly schnauzer, and I knew how she was grieving. She missed her companion of many years, and just last week she'd said she had been thinking the time might be right for another dog.

After dropping off the last of my riders that afternoon, I drove back out in my car and followed the signs. To my surprise, they led me miles back into the country, far out of our school district. I finally turned onto a dirt driveway leading up a hill to a dilapidated trailer house I was sure had to be deserted. The front door was propped open. There were no screens, and faded, tattered curtains fluttered out the windows. A door swung aimlessly on the rotting shed next to the trailer. The building was empty, and there were no signs of a car. I started to back down the drive.

Then a puppy face peeked out from under the sagging, wooden rails of the front porch. At the same time, a little girl's face popped up in an open window. I shut the car off and waited.

Both of them—the white, curly haired pup and a tiny blond girl—crept out on the porch, looking at me with wide eyes. It was plain that not too many strangers approached this place.

What Will Be

I opened the car door, and the pup tucked its tail and scooted back under the porch. The child held her ground.

"I followed the signs," I called. "I wanted to see about taking a puppy."

The little girl, who I thought was about five, just stared. She was wearing a torn shift dress with one remaining button at the neck to hold it on her thin shoulders. Her feet were bare. The only clean spot on her was the finger she had stuck in the corner of her mouth.

"Do you have any puppies to give away?" I asked.

She shook her head fiercely, her unkempt mane of straight blond hair falling like a curtain about her grimy face.

"Holly, you get that pup for the lady!" a woman's voice shrilled out the open door, and the child stiffened. "You know we can't keep it."

For a moment the girl named Holly was motionless, her face made of stone. I saw a single tear trace down her cheek, leaving a path through the dust and grime. Then she climbed down off the porch, crawled underneath on her hands and knees, and finally emerged with the scrawny, wriggling pup in her arms. She didn't offer it to me, only clutched it tightly to her thin body, while the pup madly licked her face and whimpered and wiggled.

"Holly!" I saw a shadow in the window, smoke drifting from a cigarette.

Holly slowly held the pup out to me. It was a female, some kind of curly haired terrier mix, and very small. Even though its tummy was distended with malnutrition and probably worms, it looked perfect for my sister-in-law, I thought. She loved taking in strays. But I quickly abandoned all thoughts of taking it home. How do you wrench what may be someone's only friend from their arms?

"Take it if you want it," the faceless voice instructed. "It's the last one. We can't keep it. We'll be movin' tomorrow. The mother dog got hit by a car this weekend," she added, almost as an afterthought.

Because I didn't know what else to do, I held out my arms, and Holly reluctantly handed the little pup to me. If only I could take them both! I ached all over, knowing how it must hurt this child to give up the one thing she could hold and love. I prayed the move was to a better place, a better life.

"Thank you," I said. "I'm sorry you can't keep her."

There was no response. She stared at me through the curtain of knotted hair, her face expressionless.

"She'll have a good home," I added. "She'll be loved and well fed and taken care of." I looked into the small girl's huge blue eyes, and I wanted to cry. For all the lonely little strays, not just these two.

Holly's lips trembled, the only sign she'd heard.

I sighed, got back into the car, the pup in my lap, and started down the rutted dirt drive. Then something stopped me. I shifted the car into park, opened the door, and stepped out.

"I'm going to name her Holly," I shouted. "Every time we call her, she'll remember you."

The tattered dress and the blond hair danced in the wind. She was standing just as I'd left her when I finally drove away. I realized I'd never even heard her voice.

But I'd seen the smile.

The pup did her best to wash the tears from my cheeks as I made my way down the country road.

PAYBACKS

The screams coming from somewhere across the crowded department store made me cringe. I glanced about, sure a child was either lost or hurt. Then, after a moment, I realized neither was true. This kid was screaming with pure, uncontrolled rage.

A second later, I caught sight of a white-headed, square-shouldered little boy barreling down the aisle toward me. A red-faced man, who was pretty much a larger version of the boy, was in hot pursuit.

The child looked to be about four. I knew how old the man was.

Right in front of me, the man grabbed the little kid by the arm and swept him—still screaming—off his feet.

"Hello, Frank," I called, over the child's enraged howling.

Huffing from the short sprint and the effort of hanging on to the struggling boy, the man glanced up at me with surprise.

"Uh . . . hi, Mrs. Gulley," he said. "How've you been?"

I tried not to smile too broadly as the little boy bit and scratched Frank's arm.

"Great, Frank," I answered. "Really great." I wanted to ask, "And how are you?" But it was plain that life might have hit a few snags for Frank Wallace since he'd graduated from high school just eight years ago.

I remembered how I'd looked forward to that day—the day that Frank would forever leave my bus. I'd hauled him to school since kindergarten, and I often wondered if either the bus or myself would survive to see him graduate. At the last, only sheer determination to outlive him got me through.

If a fight erupted anywhere on the bus, Frank was on the bottom of the pile. If a seat was cut, or scribbled on with pen or crayon, all the fingers pointed toward Frank. Over the years, I'd become used to having mothers call me to complain about "the Wallace kid with the snake in his pocket/squirt-gun filled with ink/cherry bombs in his boot," depending on what grade he was in.

Although he was never into any life-threatening trouble, he touched on the fringes of it . . . smoked a little pot, drank a lot of beer, and, to my everlasting sorrow, racked up a handful of speeding tickets, which kept him riding my bus until the last day of school. That last afternoon, I watched him walk away from the bus and felt a boulder crumble from my shoulders.

Now I watched in amusement as he struggled with the blond boy. I knew who this child had to be.

"Uh . . . this is Frankie, Junior," Frank told me, a weak grin on his face. "Say hi, Frankie."

The kid quit screaming long enough to stick out his tongue at me. Frank managed to keep smiling, even when little Frankie kicked him in the shin.

"He's going to start kindergarten in the fall," Frank said, attempting to set the boy on his feet, but Frankie was kicking so hard, he couldn't stand up.

"Too bad he's not on your bus route," Frank added through gritted teeth. "You're pretty good at handling spirited kids."

This time I really had to smile. Spirited? Is that what he thought he'd been?

He glanced up at me as the boy began howling anew, and I saw a funny look in his eyes. A faint and very sheepish grin spread across his face. I knew that he knew what I was thinking. He shrugged.

"Paybacks are really something," he said, gathering the wriggling child under one arm. He waved goodbye and strolled away.

I couldn't keep from laughing out loud as I heard little Frankie's shrieks disappear into the distance. *How right you are,* I thought. *Paybacks really are something.*

But really, Frank, sometimes revenge is so sweet.

RISK TAKER

"Who's that crazy person?" a voice from the back of the bus asked. I peered through the pouring rain at the figure running along the roadside. Who else would be out here training on such a cold, wet day with a thunderstorm overhead?

"Cindy!" I pulled alongside, opened the bus door, and yelled over the pounding of the rain on the metal roof. "Get in. I'll take you home."

Cindy Hanson didn't even slow down. She shook her head, her long, brown hair dripping in strings across her face. "I'm OK," she shouted back. She turned her face away from the storm and went on, mud and water splashing from her no-longer-white running shoes.

Cindy was a junior at the high school. Quiet and sweet, she was the kind of kid who fades into the woodwork, a face no one can put a name to at reunions. And while she was pretty, she tended to have a body my grandfather would have said was "built to pull a plow." I would have said "substantial."

It was only last month that I could remember ever hearing her voice. She stopped by my shoulder, blushing and uncertain. I smiled and waited.

"I won't be riding in the mornings for a while," she said so softly I could barely hear. "I'm trying out for the track team next month, and I'm going to run before school."

I know my face showed my surprise, as hard as I fought not to.

"I know," she said, turning even redder. "But if I work really hard and lose some weight . . ."

Even though I'd seen the determination on her face, I wondered how long it would last. Today, as I eased the bus past her, I felt a glimmer of excitement. Could it be she really meant to do this thing that seemed so beyond her?

"So little fat Cinderella still thinks she's going to make the track team?" Rich Castens hooted with amusement. At first the other kids on the bus hadn't cared enough about Cindy to even notice what she was doing. But we'd seen her running so many times in the past weeks that they were growing curious.

"Not with that anchor," Mark Adams laughed.

The chorus of giggles and laughter made me stiffen with anger. I felt heat rising up my neck to color my cheeks and ears. Someone behind me noticed, and I heard quick whispers and warnings. They all knew and understood that to torment a classmate on my bus was the quickest route to the superintendent's office.

The next week turned cold and windy, as well as the days following. Each morning, Cindy was there, head lowered against the biting wind, feet covered with mud, trudging down the side of the road.

It was the week after that when I began to notice something different. The talking, the general commotion began to quiet down when we spied Cindy in the distance. The kids watched silently as we passed her.

"What's *wrong* with her!" Rich's words were spoken more in wonder than as a question.

All too often, things happen on my bus that make me question why I ever wanted the job in the first place. But sometimes, God gives me a glimpse of the goodness in the kids, the wonderful adults they will become.

It happened that morning. I heard a window slide down.

"Hey, good job!" Sarah Loy yelled. "Keep it going, Cindy!"

In my side mirror, I saw Cindy glance up with surprise.

The day after, I heard an entire chorus of windows going down and a whole cheering section. "You go, girl!" "You can do it!" "Keep it going!" Hanging out the windows, banging on the side of the bus, girls and boys yelled encouragement.

The look on Cindy's face was worth the trip.

The day of the track tryouts, she was waiting for me at the end of her driveway, a gym bag slung over her shoulder. Her face was pale and unsure as she climbed the steps. Almost everyone on the bus—even the little kids in front who didn't have a clue what was going on—stood up and applauded, cheering wildly.

To my surprise, Cindy's face crumpled into tears. She plopped into a seat, her face buried in her hands.

Sarah stooped down and put her arm around Cindy's shoulders. "What's wrong?" she asked.

"I can't do this," I heard the girl's muffled sob. "What made me ever think I could do it? What if I fail? I'm going to make a fool of myself."

"Cindy, you can't let me down now." It was Rich, the world's biggest tease. And he was serious. I was stunned.

Cindy lifted her head and looked at him, confusion on her face. "Let you down?"

"I wanted all my life to go to Simpson College," he said. "But I didn't even bother to apply this spring because I thought my grades weren't good enough." He looked at the floor and stuck his hands in his pockets. "Last week, after I watched you working so hard, I filled out my application and mailed it." His face was red, and he glanced nervously around at his classmates. He wasn't used to saying anything profound.

"Yeah," Sarah said, "and I signed up for the softball team." We all stared at her. Sarah had never done anything athletic in her life.

"Well," she said, lifting her chin defiantly, "you don't know until you try."

"Yeah, and I tried out for the school play Friday." We were all in shock when Justin Ward stood up. I'd never heard him say a word, not in all the ten years he'd ridden my bus. A play?

His face was scarlet, but he didn't sit down. "I made it," he said proudly. "I've got two whole lines to say. Long lines."

"Don't you see?" Rich tried to explain. "Whatever happens, you should never think of yourself as a failure . . . because in order to fail, you have to be one of the ones who tried."

There was a trace of hope in Cindy's eyes as I put the bus in gear and headed down the road. I felt a smile spread across my face. I was suddenly glad that I was a bus driver and had the privilege of taking these kids to school.

A WASTED LIFE

Disasters flashed across my television screen tonight—a major plane crash, muggings and murders, war in a foreign country. But these things, as horrifying as they were, didn't involve me. Not directly. And although the sight of people mourning lost loved ones tore away tiny pieces of my heart, tonight my tears were not for strangers.

Tonight I cried for Tony.

A small local TV news item, insignificant to world events but devastating to those who knew. A filmed commentary of a courtroom filled with people; a quick close-up of a young man holding a baby, tears running down his flushed cheeks; stricken parents watching another young man, their only son, being led away by armed guards. Shackles on his hands and feet. Long, stringy hair hanging around his bowed head, shielding his face from the cameras.

I remembered when the hair wasn't so long, when the head was lifted in defiance to me, his dark eyes glittering with malice from a strikingly handsome twelve-year-old face.

Even then, seven years ago, I could see what was coming, the final chapter in a young wasted life.

Could any of us have written a new beginning?

Tony Martin had been a thorn in the school district's paw all his life, labeled as hyperactive and diagnosed with attention deficit and

A Wasted Life

behavioral disorders. Most of us had long ago decided his major handicap was his parents. When he became uncontrollable and someone tried any form of discipline, Tony's parents roared into the superintendent's office, complaining the current teacher/counselor/bus driver was incompetent/picking on/didn't understand their child and they wanted him moved. Not a teacher or school-bus driver escaped becoming involved in Tony's problems.

There was a time when school personnel would have taken a stand against the Martins and insisted Tony had to take responsibility for his own actions. But over the years, everyone had been simply worn down by the fight. Now there was an unspoken policy: let Tony get by with whatever he'd done, fulfill the parents' every wish, pass him no matter how bad his grades were. In short, get him through school and out of the system where he could be someone else's problem.

And that he became.

He hadn't lasted long on my bus. I'd always prided myself on being able to get along with most any kid, but Tony wasn't like any other I'd ever met. An inherent streak of pure meanness seemed to run through his otherwise intelligent mind. It seemed he couldn't perform the most simple, mundane, everyday task without adding a twist to bother or hurt someone else. When he was a little kid, a trip to the pencil sharpener meant watching him closely so he didn't yank Suzie's hair. A request to go to the bathroom couldn't be granted without a careful search to remove all crayons and sharp objects so there would be no graffiti drawn or scratched on the bathroom walls.

And then there were the slashed seats on the bus and the homework papers ripped and thrown out the rear window.

One bright fall morning, I took him by the arm and escorted him to a front seat.

"Until you can act with some small semblance of respect and maturity, you'll be sitting here," I snarled at him, knowing he didn't have a clue what I was talking about and cared even less.

"I don't have to sit here," he hissed back, adding an obscene remark. "You can't make me!"

"Just watch me!" I said, writing out a misconduct slip. I was so mad the writing was all squiggled from my shaking hands.

The Martins beat me back to the bus garage after I let Tony off at the junior high. He must have walked directly to the phone . . . right after he'd turned around and shouted an obscene name at me.

"She's picking on Tony!" they shouted at my boss, Mac. "We won't stand for him being treated this way. We want him put on another bus. He's sick. He's on medication. She's upsetting him!"

They ignored me as though I wasn't the adult, as though Tony hadn't been in trouble with every bus driver in the system, as though their anger and shouting could save their son.

Mac looked at me, a pained, long-suffering expression on his face, and raised his eyebrows into question marks. A moment of resentment sifted through my thoughts, that Mac would shift this decision to my shoulders, as though the kid was all mine to deal with. What about him? Couldn't he tell the Martins he was the transportation director and that he was the one who would decide the appropriate action?

Should I protest and try to make the Martins see how this was harming their son? Should I plead with them to talk to yet another doctor or counselor . . . someone who could make them understand what was happening?

I looked into their flushed and angry faces. And I shrugged. In front of them, I tore the misconduct slip into tiny pieces.

"If they think Tony will get along better on another bus, then do it," I said. Mac was more than happy to. He'd dealt with the Martins before.

God forgive me, I was delighted.

In that same manner, Tony was shoved through the system, each of us too tired, too burned out, to deal with his problems. We let him slip away quietly and with as few ripples as possible. Now the law was doing the dealing and all the cards were on the table.

Tony and several friends had attacked a stranded motorist, beaten her viciously, and taken her car. She'd died a day later, leaving behind a husband and a two-month-old baby.

His parents cried and argued before the judge, carrying on their life's vocation, pleading that their son had merely gotten in with a bad crowd.

A Wasted Life

"Mr. and Mrs. Martin," the judge told them quietly. "Tony *is* the bad crowd."

At last someone was forcing them to take a responsibility they'd long avoided.

All my life, it has been my character to shoulder all the guilt of the world. But today, as I watched the faces of Tony's parents filled with helpless confusion and terror, I knew the guilt was shared: the school, the teachers, the drivers. It belonged to each of us. We allowed that young woman to be killed. Left her husband a widower and her baby without a mother.

And we destroyed Tony.

It was so easy. All we had to do was nothing.

REMEMBER

I don't know why I stopped my school bus at Jed Cooper's driveway that morning. It was the last day of March, a soft warm day that held a hint of spring, and I was so lost in thought, I even turned on the overhead warning flashers. The kids behind me had never been so quiet. I could even hear the *click-click, click-click* as the bright red and yellow lights blinked merrily. We all gazed up the lane, waiting, every one of us knowing that Jed was not going to be walking down to meet the bus. Not today. Not ever again.

It had been four months since Jed died. I didn't like to think about it much. It had been crazy kid stuff that went wrong—a few beers, a fast pickup truck, rites of passage that most teenagers survive. Except the pickup had been stolen, as had the money to buy the beer. To be fair, it had been an old truck, rusted and parked probably forever behind a neighbor's barn. And the money was a few dollars left lying on the counter of the fast-food joint by a careless waitress. Typical of the stuff Jed pulled. Not horrible, just half-bad.

Still, a lot of people hadn't been at all surprised when they heard about the wreck. Jed's lifetime track record hadn't been exactly spotless. There was lots of trouble in school—suspensions, poor grades, the usual, and more. Sometimes he hadn't been a joy to me on the bus, either. But still, I had some very good memories of him. It made me smile when I thought of the devilish grin that split his freckled face from ear to ear. He'd had dark eyes that seemed to spit sparks whenever he had foolishness plotted. He teased the little kids unmercifully, but when one of them needed a buddy, Jed was right there to help or just sympathize. It was the same with the kids his age. I'd watched him taunt and poke fun at an unhappy friend, until the other kid had to cheer up in self-defense, if nothing else.

I didn't know why at the end, Jed had done what he did. I could only trust that God had been kind to him. I was determined to believe there'd been a lot of good in Jed Cooper.

As I finally shifted the bus into gear and started to pull away from the Cooper driveway, I caught a glimpse of the woman kneeling in the flowerbed in the front yard. Jed's mother. She was staring at us, and clear from the road, I could see the haunted look on her face.

"Tomorrow is Jed's birthday," a little grade-school boy said out of the blue.

"How do you know that?" I asked.

" 'Cause Jed told me he was an April fool," the boy said, grinning as he remembered.

I smiled too. It was exactly something Jed would say.

I thought about the look on Mrs. Cooper's face. Then I had an idea.

"Let's give Jed a birthday card," I said, to no one particular. In the big overhead mirror, I saw several surprised faces look up at me.

"How will we give it to him?" one of the little kids asked seriously.

"We'll give it to his mom," I said. "If there's something really neat you remember about Jed, write it in a letter tonight," I added on impulse. "We'll put the notes in with the card."

The older ones looked at me like I was crazy, but all the grade-schoolers were excited. That night I picked out a pretty card with bright balloons, a big one with lots of space for writing. The next morning I passed it around the bus.

At the high school, one of Jed's friends brought the card up to me. It was scribbled from top to bottom with names—some written in flowing script, some printed in big, shaky block letters. And it was stuffed with letters of every size and description. After I dropped off the last of the kids, I read a few of the notes.

"Jed, thanks for making me laugh."

"Hey, Jed! We miss you at the track."

"You were my friend when no one else wanted to hang around with me. Thanks."

I tucked everything into the envelope and drove it out to the Cooper's mailbox.

It wasn't until later that day I began to worry about whether I'd done the right thing. Maybe it was too many memories too soon. Maybe instead of making Mrs. Cooper feel better, it would only serve to hurt her.

As the day went on, I agonized more and more. On the afternoon bus run, when I saw Jed's mom waiting by the mailbox, my heart almost stopped. The look on her face turned a knife deep in my chest. There were tears running down her cheeks, and her mouth was twisted and trembling.

I knew for sure the card had been a mistake.

The bus was silent as I pulled to a stop and opened the door. Behind me, I could see big, frightened eyes watching as Mrs. Cooper climbed the steps.

"Mrs. Cooper," I said, "I'm sorry if we upset you."

She didn't say anything for a long time, just gazed from face to face. Then her voice was almost a whisper.

"I know Jed was a troublemaker. When he died, I thought, maybe, that a lot of people were . . ." she swallowed painfully. "I thought a lot of people might be kind of . . . well, glad. I was feeling so awful today," she continued. "Then I found this card in my mailbox."

She held it up for everyone to see.

"It was just like God had reached down to tell me that no one is ever forgotten, that no one is all bad."

She stared at the kids for another long moment, tears streaming down her face.

"Thank you," she said and smiled.

FORGIVING

The bright red car in the high-school parking lot reflected the afternoon sun like a mirror. It was waxed to a perfect shine, obviously cared for and cherished. It was also surrounded by glittering shards of broken glass. Where the windshield should have been was a jagged, gaping hole.

I knew who the car belonged to—Bryan Easton, a senior boy who was more into fast cars and late nights than studies or sports. And I knew someone was going to pay dearly for this vandalism. I swung the bus wide, avoiding the bits of glass scattered everywhere like snow, and pulled up in front of the school doors. The kids were ominously silent as they got on the bus.

A tall, thin, blond senior boy climbed the steps and hesitated next to me, his eyes on the battered car. Even though they seemed to be direct opposites, Rich Lamont was Bryan's best friend. In contrast to Bryan's late nights and rumored drinking and wild driving, Rich loved to read and took great pride in his grades. He preferred studying to cruising with the guys in the evenings. But I often watched the two boys talk and laugh together. Rich was tolerant of Bryan's king-of-the-mountain ways, and Bryan, in turn, respected Rich's desire to do things right. They'd been buddies since kindergarten.

This morning, as we stared at the battered car, Rich's voice was so quiet I could barely hear. "I sure wouldn't want to be the one who did that," he said. The words trembled just the least little bit, and I looked up at him.

"Do you have any ideas?" I asked.

He shook his head, looking down at the floor. "Someone did it at lunch," he said. "No one saw it. I feel sorry for the person who did it when Bryan finds him." His words echoed my thoughts.

"And when I find out, they're gonna die. Know what I mean?" The voice behind us was hard and angry and filled with violence. Both Rich and I jumped. Bryan was standing at the bottom of the bus steps, a hand on either side of the door, his square frame filling the doorway. His black hair fell across his face, the heavy dark eyebrows pulled together in the middle of his face like a gathering thunderstorm. The veins stood out in the back of his hands.

Bryan wasn't a person you'd want to cross. He'd ridden my bus for years before he was old enough for the car, and even as a child, he'd intimidated most of the other kids. He wasn't a mean kid, just intense and ready to take up a full-scale war against anyone who dared to do something he didn't like.

Rich just looked at him. Bryan walked up the steps, his first bus ride in two years, and the two boys went to the back seats. I could hear Bryan grumbling all the way.

"Larson's Body Shop is going to come out and get it and fix the windshield," he told Rich. "It'll take forever to clean the glass out of it. When I catch the jerk who did it . . ."

Rich was the last kid off my bus each evening. That night it seemed to take him forever to walk down the aisle when I pulled to a stop at the end of his driveway. He stood for a long moment at the open door, staring out into the country. Then he stepped outside and walked down the driveway without a glance back.

I wondered if he really did know who'd done the damage to Bryan's car and for some reason was afraid to tell. Over the years, Bryan and Rich had weathered the normal tiffs and arguments, but they'd been buddies since kindergarten. It was hard to think of anything coming between them.

I didn't have a clue.

The next morning, when I pulled the bus into the high-school parking lot, Rich lagged behind until the rest of the kids were out-

Forgiving

side, headed for the school doors. When he stopped next to me, I looked up. I was stunned to see how pale his face was. He made no move to get off the bus.

"Mrs. Gulley?" When he finally spoke, his voice was quiet but resolute. "Could I talk to you?"

I'd suspected all along that Rich knew who'd damaged Bryan's car. I turned off the key and looked up, prepared to hear the name of the culprit. Rich wouldn't look at me. He stared intently at the ground. What he said took my breath away.

"It was me. I did it."

I had no words. I couldn't even believe that I'd heard correctly. My mouth moved, but no sound came out. Then I took a deep breath and tried again.

"You? Do you mean you're the one who smashed Bryan's windshield?"

He nodded miserably.

"But . . . but why, Rich? You guys are friends."

He looked up then, and all he could do was shrug, his eyes filled with misery.

I took another deep breath, trying to think this through.

"You have to tell Bryan," I said finally.

He nodded again, his head bowed. He looked like an unhappy third-grader.

"Let's go talk to Principal Anderson," I said. "He'll know what you need to do."

As we walked into the school office, my mind was whirling. Principal Anderson took one look at Rich's white face and ushered us into his office, closing the door behind us.

"What can I do for you, Rich?" he asked gently.

The boy buried his face in his hands, his shoulders shaking. Somehow he managed to repeat his story.

The principal buzzed the outside office. "Please send Bryan Easton down," he asked. Rich seemed to shrink smaller and smaller as the moments went by. When Bryan opened the office door and stepped inside, Rich leaped to his feet, almost tipping his chair over in the process. Bryan's face was puzzled as he looked from Rich to Mr. Anderson to me.

111

"What's up?" he asked cautiously.

Principal Anderson sighed. "We know who damaged your car," he said.

The anger on Bryan's face was frightening. "Who?" he rumbled, his dark eyes narrowing to slits. "Who was it?"

We were frozen, none of us able to answer. And from our silence, Bryan knew. He turned to Rich, and for a long moment, he stared at his friend, his shoulders rising and falling with breaths of rage.

"*You?*" he whispered. "*You?*" The boy's hands doubled into fists, the knuckles white. I stepped forward to grab him, afraid he was going to lash out. But what he did next blew my mind away.

Tears brimmed in Bryan's eyes. He held his hands out helplessly toward his friend.

"But why, Rich?" he whispered, his voice soft and wounded.

"I don't know," Rich cried out, his own eyes filling with tears. "I don't know. There were other guys there . . . they kept telling me, 'Do it; do it.' I don't know why. I'm sorry, Bryan. I . . ." His voice trailed off. He covered his face with his hands again.

Bryan took a breath all the way from the tips of his toes. Then he stepped forward and put his arm around Rich's shoulders.

"Hey, man," he said. "It's just a car. We can fix it. There are things in life we can't do anything about, but a stupid windshield is no problem. Know what I mean?"

Rich didn't look up. He gulped and sighed, and then I saw him nod.

The two boys left to go back to class. I watched them walk down the hall, saw Bryan hesitate and then turn back to us.

"Rich's dad has cancer," he said quietly. "He isn't going to make it. Sometimes living with a thing like that makes a guy do some crazy stuff. Know what I mean?"

After twenty years of driving a bus, dealing with kids on a daily basis, I'd seen a lot of things that made me wonder about the future of the world. Watching Bryan Easton, our school "bad boy" walk down the hall that morning, I knew our future was in far better hands than I'd thought.

Bryan knew he couldn't fix the world, but he was trying to fix what he could.

Section 5

Fears, Tears, and Summer Dreams

EVERY THORN HAS A ROSE

I braked my school bus to a stop at Caleb Beck's driveway and pulled open the door. There was silence on the bus as the kids stared out at the elderly man standing in his devastated flower garden. The man could have been a scarecrow propped up there, in his patched overalls and standard checked farmer shirt. He leaned heavily on his rake and stared back, his lined, weathered face showing no sign of either warmth or welcome.

"I'm not doing this," Danny Wilson breathed behind me. I looked back and lifted my eyebrows at the short, stocky freshman. His dark hair and heavy brows made him look more sinister than I knew he was. And I knew the stubborn frown on his square face would do him no good whatsoever. He was going to do it, all right. A judge in our small town had told him so.

Danny was not a bad kid, just a kid with bad judgment. He and several of his friends, cruising with nothing in particular to do, had skidded their old car into Caleb's immaculately tended front yard and pretty much obliterated his beautiful flower garden.

Danny had lived next door to Caleb for all of his fifteen years, and he'd been a thorn in the old man's side for most of that time. His escapades ranged from running through the garden as a mischievous grade-school kid to last year's prank of soaping the old farmhouse's windows on Halloween night.

Every Thorn Has a Rose

"Ah, they needed it," Danny had whined to me. "The old goat hasn't washed his windows since the dinosaurs walked by."

Not bad stuff, just an irritation. Until now. I knew how much the flowers meant to Caleb.

The judge knew too. "One hundred hours of community service," he'd ordered, and then told Danny that his hours would be served in Caleb Beck's front yard.

Now I waited, and Caleb waited while Danny finally made up his mind there was no way out.

With a sigh, looking as though he were going to attend his own funeral, he stood up and walked down the bus steps.

At the bottom, he hesitated, then turned around. "If I don't come back," he said, "I want my seat to go to Connie Foster. With a body like hers, she deserves it." Even the little kids laughed.

I shut the door, trying not to laugh with them. Danny needed to know everyone, both young and old, has feelings. I wondered if he ever thought about it. Or cared.

He didn't have much to say the next morning. He avoided my eyes and stomped back to his seat.

"So, how are you getting along with Mr. Beck?" I finally asked.

Judging by the angry flush that spread across the teen's face, not well.

"I had to dig up the whole garden," he grumbled. " Even the roses. Do you know they have thorns like needles? And he's going to make me reseed the whole thing. I had to take three showers to get all the dirt off. And I have a blister the size of Texas."

"Oh, that's too bad," I said, trying not to laugh. "Sounds like hard work."

"You bet," Danny agreed, totally missing my sarcasm. "But the hardest part is listening to him rattle on. All he talks about is when he fought in the stupid war. He never shuts up. And he can't hear a thing when I talk to him."

"Maybe he just needs someone to talk to," I said.

"He talks to those dumb flowers," the boy told me. "The old goat's crazy."

I frowned at him.

"OK, OK," Danny said. "Mr. *Beck* is crazy."

I sighed, fearing for the future of our world with a kid like this to take over.

As the days went by, I began to notice Caleb Beck was always in the yard when I pulled up with the bus. In fact, I could see him looking for us when I turned the corner off the highway. A smile lit up his face when Danny reluctantly climbed down the bus steps. It was almost as though the elderly man was looking forward to his confrontations with this mouthy teen.

"You back again, punk?" I heard him say.

"Only because I have to, you old goat," Danny replied under his breath.

"Danny!" I whispered sharply.

"What?" Caleb shouted.

"Yeah, yeah," Danny shouted. "I'm back." He turned to look at me, made a face, and trudged across the yard to his doom.

I was curious one afternoon when Danny carried a huge book onto the bus from the school library and buried his nose in it throughout the ride home.

"That book must really be interesting," I remarked just before he got off the bus. His face turned red again, but this time with embarrassment.

"It's a history of World War II," he admitted. "There's some neat stuff in here. Did you know Old Man Beck was on the *Arizona* during the attack on Pearl Harbor? He says he lost the hearing in his right ear when there was an explosion close to him."

I winced at the reference to "Old Man Beck" but then decided it hadn't really been spoken in a mean way. And I was amazed that Danny actually knew something about a historical event.

"Yes, I did," I told him. "Makes it kind of up close and personal, doesn't it?"

The boy didn't answer, but his eyes were thoughtful, an unusual occurrence with this kid.

I watched the flower garden take shape over the next month. Danny spaded and raked and pulled weeds, moaning and complaining the whole way. But every now and then he mentioned something to me about the past war that he found particularly fascinating.

"Did you know Mr. Beck had a son?" he asked one morning.

"No, I didn't know that," I said, too surprised to even comment on his use of *Mr. Beck*.

"Yeah, his name was Jamie. He was killed in Vietnam. He was only eighteen." Danny swallowed painfully. "Caleb planted the flower garden as a memorial to him." He said it matter-of-factly, but he seemed to get off the bus more quickly after that.

Green poked through the black, carefully raked earth, plants began to grow, a flower bloomed. Danny pointed it out to me with great pride.

"That's a crocus," he said. "They're a bulb. They're one of the first to bloom." He showed me the calluses on his hands and the black earth ground under his fingernails. "Those roses will bloom later."

I had to look up, to see if this was really the same Danny Wilson who several months ago would have been appalled at the idea of dirt on his hands. That Danny wouldn't have had a clue what a bulb was, much less a crocus or a rose.

But it was on a Friday in June, the last day of school, when the teenager removed all doubt from my mind about what the future held for our world.

He'd told me earlier in the week that his community hours were done Thursday. He'd fulfilled his obligation to the court. So on Friday afternoon, I sailed right on by the Beck house.

"Mrs. Gulley," Danny yelled. "Stop!"

Confused, I hit the brakes. The boy was already at my shoulder as I opened the door.

"But I thought your community service hours were all done," I said.

The teen shrugged and grinned. "Are they?" he asked. "How about that."

Across the yard, Caleb Beck waited. I could see his face light up when I opened the bus door.

"Get over here and get to work, you long-haired punk," the old man cackled, his face creased in a huge smile.

"Don't get your drawers in an uproar, you old goat," Danny shouted back. "He'd kill those roses in a heartbeat," he said to me under his breath. "Doesn't have a clue how to cut them back." Then he grinned again, winked, and trotted across the yard to the old man.

DRAGON SLAYER

It always made me nervous when I found Principal Anderson waiting for me as I pulled my school bus into the high school. It usually wasn't to tell me good news. I could see today was probably no exception. His eyes looked tired, his face tight with a hint of annoyance.

"We have a new student starting next Monday," he said after I opened the bus door to let the kids out. "He has a disablity, and I'm afraid we'll have to switch you over to another bus."

I knew what bus he was talking about: number seventeen, a used vehicle we'd had for several years. It was equipped with a special lift to load a wheelchair. In poor repair and probably not even usable, the lift served to bring the district into compliance with the federal accessibility codes. Our small school system had never had to accommodate a wheelchair student, a blessing in more ways than one.

Principal Anderson sighed. "He's in seventh grade," he added. "We have to construct a ramp to the middle school entrance and remodel the boys' bathroom. Plus, I think, the cafeteria door and lunch line will have to be redesigned."

The antiquated junior-high building had no ground-level entrance. The school itself badly needed to be replaced. Now expensive changes had to be made. Necessary changes, but still taxing the reserves of a school system already suffering an overburdened budget.

I sympathized with the look on the principal's face. Old number seventeen wasn't my choice of buses to drive, and I didn't have a clue how to work the lift.

But by Monday morning, the construction of a new ramp had begun, plans were being drawn for the lunchroom changes, and I was headed out into the country with one quick lesson in hydraulic lift operation under my belt.

None of the preparations could have prepared us for Alan Hasselroth.

My bus kids weren't happy about switching to the old, noisy bus, and each one had a complaint as they walked up the steps. But the moans and groans faded to silence as we pulled up to the Hasselroth driveway. A small, dark-headed boy in a wheelchair was struggling down the gravel lane. Even from where I sat, I could see the sweat on his forehead as he negotiated the bumpy path.

We watched for a moment. I didn't know what to do.

"Let me out. I'll help." The voice behind me was Ross Miller, the biggest football player on the varsity squad. He trotted down the drive while I busied myself trying to figure out the wheelchair lift.

"To the coach, my man!" the voice cried. Alan was waving his arms about and pointing in the direction of the bus. "I'll make sure the king rewards you most handsomely." Ross, who had really never had much of a sense of humor, surprised me by grinning as he pushed the chair up to the bus.

On closer inspection, Alan wasn't as small as he'd appeared. His broad shoulders were muscular, as were his upper arms and hands. The dark eyes peering out from under a shock of even darker hair were wide and bright. Somehow this kid didn't fit my idea of "physically challenged."

"Ah, there you are," Alan said. "I was afraid this sixty-passenger pumpkin had no driver."

"Fear no more, kind sir," I teased. "Your chariot awaits and your driver, Mrs. Gulley by name, is at your disposal." I bowed as I pushed the remote and prayed. The lift cranked noisily and shrieked with metal against metal as it lowered halfway to the ground. And there it stuck.

Dragon Slayer

"Well, Driver Gulley," Alan said, grinning as he surveyed the cranky lift. "It looks as though getting me aboard today will be a bit of a tussle."

A tussle to say the least. The temperamental lift refused to come down. With the help of several more senior football players we managed to get it back into the bus. Then we bodily carried Alan up the front steps while others stuffed the wheelchair in through the back door. When at last he was seated and secured I noticed the beads of sweat had popped out on his face again. The whole affair had been hard work for him, too.

"I'm sorry," I apologized. "I promise I'll get the hang of this. Sorry to make it such a problem."

"Problems are my life," he said. "This happens a lot. It's OK." His smile was sincere.

When we pulled into the middle school, the procedure was reversed, except this time Alan had to be carried up the school steps into the front hallway. He maintained his sense of humor and cheerful attitude through it all. I knew the difficulty with the bathrooms and the lunchroom was still ahead, and I was embarrassed by our lack of preparation—mine, the school's, the district's. How could we have worried about the bother and expense of accommodating this boy when even under the best of conditions, his days were difficult? I knew I was getting a small glimpse of what hard work life is for a person with disabilities in a world made for nondisabled people.

That afternoon, Alan had a crowd around him as he was carried out to the bus. He was waving a cardboard sword and carrying a bicycle helmet that could be mistaken for a knight's suit of armor— if you had a great imagination.

Strong young hands lifted him into the bus and down the aisle, while others pushed and pulled the wheelchair into the back. They were all there to help when we reached the Hasselroth driveway, and I just stood out of the way, not minding the commotion one bit. It was good to see the kids on my bus so concerned with a fellow classmate.

"Hey, Alan," I called as two classmates helped him negotiate the gravel lane. "What's with the sword and helmet?"

He turned around and leaned over the side of the wheelchair.

"I'm Sir Lancelot in the school play," he yelled back. "They had to give me the part—I'm permanently attached to this horse."

It made me smile. *What a wonderful addition to our school,* I thought. A kid like Alan brought out the wonderful things in everyone. And how fitting he should play Sir Lancelot.

After all, he spent every day of his life slaying dragons.

UNDERNEATH IT ALL

"No-o-o!" The high-pitched wail from the middle of the school bus was so distressed it made cold chills run up and down my arms, even though it was September and the temperature was well over eighty. I knew immediately who it was, and I was pretty sure I knew who and what had caused her to scream.

Gritting my teeth, I stepped on the brake and pulled to the side of the road. The hysterical sobbing continued as I unbuckled my seat belt and stood up. "Tony!" I said as calmly as I could manage, considering the commotion going on, "Give it back! Now!" The squared-faced middle-school boy next to the window flushed a bright red and threw the wool ski cap he was holding back across the aisle. The tiny kindergarten girl in the seat was crying so hard she didn't even notice.

"Mandi," I said, bending down next to her. "Mandi, it's OK. Here. Tony gave your cap back." She snuffled a hiccup, grabbed the wool cap, and pulled it down over her fuzz-covered, nearly bald head. With shaking fingers clutched tight, she held on with a death grip, tears still running down her pale cheeks. Her huge blue eyes stared up at me from under the cap, and the terror there was very real—much too bright for a five-year-old.

"Mandi," I whispered. "You're such a pretty girl. Why don't you take your hat off today? It's too hot to wear it anyway." Mandi jammed the hat down to her eyebrows and shook her head. She sank into the corner of her seat, letting me know the discussion was at an end.

I sighed and turned to Tony. He also sank into his seat, smiling up at me hopefully, while he tried to disappear. "Sorry," he said, "I didn't know she was going to go crazy over that stupid hat."

"Leave her alone," I said, enunciating each word with great care so there would be no mistake. "Do not under any circumstances touch her or that cap again." I raised my eyebrows in an expression I saved for special occasions. Tony nodded quickly. The look on his face was so sincere, I almost laughed. He wasn't a bad kid, I knew. Just a typical junior-high boy—from his fashionably oversized denim shirt right down to his untied basketball shoes with fluorescent laces—and right now he'd agree to anything I said just to stay out of trouble. However, I also knew the minute I turned my back, all previous agreements went out the window.

I wondered if he'd be any different if he knew more about Mandi. What would he say if I announced that the little kindergartener hiding in the bus seat could tell him all he ever wanted to know about leukemia? That all summer while he'd been playing baseball with his friends and jumping his bike over garbage cans in the backyard, she'd lain in a hospital bed struggling with chemotherapy treatments? Being constantly weak and sick to her stomach hadn't seemed to get her down, her mother told me, but Mandi cried big silent tears when her beautiful long blond hair began to fall out in clumps.

Now the disease was in remission. For the moment, Mandi had a future, but all that concerned her was that her hair was gone—her pretty hair. The day she'd come home from the hospital, she'd found the winter cap in her dresser. She'd pulled it over her bare head, and there it stayed, despite pleading, cajoling, and even threats from the adults in her world. Even the teasing from the school kids hadn't made a difference. I sighed and went back to my seat. I'd learned long ago that life wasn't always fair, but knowing didn't make acceptance one bit easier.

As we neared the grade school, I was aware of something going on in the middle section of the bus. I stopped at the front doors and looked into the overhead mirror, prepared to nail Tony to the wall this time if he'd dared put a hand on Mandi's hat. He had. His face was redder than ever, and he squirmed in his seat as he waited to see what I would do. As Mandi skipped down the aisle, my plans for Tony changed. I saw a big hug in his future.

Mandi's eyes were big and round and filled with pride. For the first time, a smile dimpled her little cheeks. "Look!" she cried with delight. "I'm pretty!" The cap was gone. In its place, tied into a clumsy big bow around her fuzzy head, was one of Tony's bright yellow shoe-laces.

NOT LIKE ME

The tall, lanky boy avoided my eyes as he slouched up the steps of the bus, running one hand through his dark, unruly hair. In my overhead rearview mirror, I watched him swagger to the back where the middle-school kids sat. He paused next to Danny Hixson, and the little first-grader ducked down into the seat, his hands covering his head. The older boy glanced up to see if I was watching.

"Cody!" I warned. "Sit down."

The boy shrugged and slid into his own seat, postponing whatever devilment he'd planned. He smiled a huge, fake smile at me, all his white teeth showing. I didn't smile back.

Thirteen-year-old Cody Bowman had never been a real problem on my school bus, but he was the kind I always watched closely. I couldn't help it. I'd grown up in a time when long, greasy hair, ragged jeans, and a dirty T-shirt marked a kid as trouble. Cody also came equipped with a mouth that was more than a little too quick, but even though he was usually involved in almost any disruption in the junior-high section of the bus, I really hadn't labeled him as "bad." Not yet.

The Bowmans had moved into the run-down farmhouse on my bus route less than a year earlier, along with a colorful assortment of junk cars in the driveway and two or three hounds tied to unpainted doghouses in the yard. I knew Cody's mom and dad both worked long hours in town, leaving him alone most of the day. I also knew

126

kids like Cody, with nothing much to do and no adult supervision, have a tough time staying out of trouble.

Over the months, I'd watched the expression on his face become sneaky and sly, watched his little-kid walk turn into an obnoxious swagger, so typical of an eighth-grader. I listened to my own voice call his name more and more often. I handed him one "bad conduct" slip after another, assuring him many nights in detention hall, but nothing seemed to change. I worried about him.

That afternoon, when I pulled to a stop at the end of the Bowman driveway, I found a new worry. A huge, evil-looking black motorcycle was parked next to the junked cars. A heavyset man—an older, bearded, carbon-copy of Cody—stood by the front door of the house.

"My brother's here!" Cody whooped as he leaped over the steps out of the bus and raced down the driveway. "Hi Jonathan!" I heard him shout.

I glanced toward the house at the man. He hadn't moved. His unkempt beard and long, shaggy hair whipped around his face in the breeze. Dressed in ripped jeans, engineer boots that had been out of style for years, and a formerly white T-shirt now covered with oil, he looked like a reincarnation of a fifties "hoodlum." But I knew this man was no one to make fun of. His dark eyes, shadowed by massive black brows, burned with a message I couldn't read. Cody raced to the stranger, and when I pulled away, they were happily doing guy things—punching shoulders, parrying and dancing like prize fighters, as they greeted one another.

From then on, each night when the bus pulled to a stop, the big man raised his huge upper body from deep within the engine of whatever vehicle he'd been working on . . . and watched. And my nagging worry turned inward.

His stare was so accusing. What had I done? Did he resent my more-and-more reluctant efforts to discipline Cody? It was almost as though he was daring me . . . daring me to . . . what? The icy look sent chills up and down my spine.

On a cold, cloudy afternoon, Cody once again pushed me past the limits of my patience—and my fear.

"Mrs. Gulley!" a little voice cried. "Cody threw my folder out the window."

I glanced up. Papers fluttered down the gravel road behind us. Suzie, a quiet second-grader, clutched the back of the seat, tears spilling down her cheeks. I pulled to the side of the road. The bus was silent.

"Cody," I said. "That was mean."

"It was an accident," the boy smirked. "They slipped." He basked in the muffled giggles from the kids around him.

I told him to come up and sit in the seat behind me with the little kids—the ultimate punishment for an eighth-grader. It gave me a great sense of satisfaction to see pink patches of embarrassment stain his cheeks as he sat down. Then I wrote out yet another bad conduct slip and handed it to him. He stared back at me defiantly.

I sighed. "You know your parents have to sign this and you have to give it back to me in the morning if you want to ride the bus," I said. "Then your principal will deal with you. I expect you'll be spending a few more nights in detention hall, Cody, since you've had plenty of these slips this year."

Cody's face darkened. "We'll see about that," he muttered. I thought about the man in the yard, and I had to work hard to hold back a little shiver. *It doesn't matter,* I told myself bravely. *The kid deserves this and more. He has to learn he can't get away with this kind of behavior.*

But the next morning, when I saw the bearded man standing beside Cody in the driveway, my knees were so weak I could hardly get the bus braked to a stop.

Arguments were already running through my mind, as I swung the door open. Statements with which to defend myself. But somehow, when I stared into the angry black eyes, I was desperately mute.

The man shoved Cody forward.

"Tell her!" he ordered in a voice to match his size, so full of gravelly anger that I cringed.

What a coward I was! Determinedly, I squared my shoulders ready to do battle with both of them. *The discipline slips are for Cody's own good,* I thought. I gripped the steering wheel tightly so they couldn't see my fingers shaking.

Not Like Me

"I'm sorry." Cody's voice was so soft I wasn't sure I'd heard.

"What?" I gasped.

"Louder!" the man rasped.

"I'm sorry," Cody repeated, handing me a stack of neatly folded papers. I looked down. They were the contents of Suzie's folder, each page painstakingly wiped clean.

I looked back at Cody, my mind whirling.

"My little brother won't be giving you any more trouble," the big man said. He squeezed Cody's shoulder, and I saw the smaller boy wince. "If he does anything more that you don't like—anything at all—let me know. I'll take care of it." He smiled, and his homely, hairy face was suddenly transformed into that of a shy little boy.

"I was a troublemaker, too, when I was in school," he went on. "Thought I was pretty hot stuff . . . didn't need no books or classes."

He nodded at Cody, his face turning serious again. "I'm going to make sure he can do something for a living besides fixin' junk cars. Don't want him to turn out like me."

All I could do was stare at him, my mouth hanging open. Cody walked to the back of the bus and slipped into his seat—quietly. Still speechless, I put the bus in gear and headed down the road. But as my thoughts gathered together, I felt a smile spread across my face. I knew someday I'd tell Jonathan that I surely hoped his little brother would indeed, turn out to be exactly like him.

Loving and caring are marvelous traits for brothers to share.

KINDERGARTEN STARFISH

I'd just dropped off the last of my kids at the grade school when I saw the little blond-headed boy burst through the kindergarten door on the run. He flew down the sidewalk, and I could tell he was making a break for freedom. As I leaped down the bus steps, intending to give chase, Elsie Morino, the kindergarten teacher, charged through the doors after him. Just before he reached the street, she had him by the collar and dragged him to a stop. She took his hand and tried to pull him toward the school. He gritted his teeth and braced himself, his heels skidding on the sidewalk.

"Rusty," Elsie panted, her long, gray-streaked hair falling across her face. "You get back in your room right now or I'll take you to see Principal Anderson."

"I don't care," the little kid screamed, struggling to get away. "I don't want to go back. You can't make me."

I hurried over and took his other hand. "Come on, Rusty," I said. "Let's go."

Faced with two adults, Rusty gave up the fight. He pouted all the way into the school and back to his room. When she had him safely sitting at his desk and the class occupied momentarily with a coloring-book project, Elsie slipped out into the hall with me and shut the door behind her. She took a deep breath, tucking long strands of hair behind her ears, wiping the sweat from her forehead. With the back of her hand she scrubbed at her eyes.

"I'm sorry," she sniffled. "I'm just so discouraged. I spend more time trying to maintain order with this class than I do teaching."

"I can relate to that," I said. I sympathized with her. Things had changed on my school bus over the years, too, I told her. It seemed as though many of the kids no longer felt the adult was the authority figure. Respect for the person in charge was pretty much a thing of the past.

"I have only eighteen children in this class," Elsie said. "Would you believe twelve of them are from divorced homes? And another family is in the process of separating." She nodded her head at the door. "Rusty's family."

"A sign of the times," I said. "A very sad sign. It's just too bad that these little ones are the victims, the ones that suffer the most."

She nodded again in agreement and sighed, then turned around to stare through the glass panel in the door. Inside the children were already growing bored with what they were doing; I saw one little girl reach over and scribble a red line across her neighbor's drawing. The other kindergartener retaliated with a blue crayon. An angry scream echoed out into the hall.

"I have to go back in there," Elsie said, in a tone that made me believe it was the last thing in the world she wanted to do. She hesitated and looked at me again. "I used to wake up in the morning and actually be excited about going to work," she added. "I loved being a teacher. Now I lie in bed, staring at the ceiling, and wonder if I really want to do this anymore."

"The school needs good teachers like you," I told her. "Maybe this is just an unusual class of kids. Things will be better next year."

She chuckled, but there was no mirth in the sound. "I don't think so. It's been going downhill for a number of years now. But," she rubbed her hands across her face, "I keep praying for patience. And I keep searching for the starfish in each class."

For a moment, I was puzzled. Then I smiled as I remembered the well-worn story of the boy walking down a beach where thousands of starfish had been washed up by the tide. He was throwing them back into the sea, one by one. A passerby asked him why he bothered to do it. "There are so many of them," the man said. "What difference can it possibly make?"

The boy picked up one more and said, "It makes a difference to this one," and threw it into the sea.

"Do you always find one?" I asked Elsie.

"Once in a while," she said, her smile brightening. "This year it's been tough, though. I guess I'll just keep praying."

She thanked me again for my help and went back to her class. The expression on her face must have been similar to the look on the Christians going in to face the lions. With a couple of major differences: these were baby lions, much more frightening. And the Christians had to face the terror only once. I said a silent prayer for her.

That afternoon, as the kids were climbing into their buses to go home, Elsie walked back to me. Her eyes betrayed her feelings. The day hadn't gone well.

"I had to call Principal Anderson in to keep order this afternoon," she said. "We were trying to play a game, and two of the boys fought over a chair. One threw a book at the other and cracked a window."

She took a deep breath and ran her fingers through her long hair. "What am I going to do?" Her voice trembled. "Maybe I just wasn't cut out to be a teacher. Maybe God is trying to tell me I need to give this up."

Before I could answer, a tall, thin young woman walked up to us. The little blond boy she held by the hand was all too familiar.

"Hello, Rusty," Elsie said.

"Are you Mrs. Morino?" the woman asked.

Elsie nodded, glancing up at me as though to make sure she had a backup if this turned ugly.

I was stunned to see the young woman's eyes fill with tears. "I'm so glad to meet you," she said. "I'm Rusty's mother, and I've wanted to tell you how much I appreciate all the time you've spent with him. You can't imagine how much it's helped him at home. I've seen such a difference in him since he's been in your class."

I wanted to tell Elsie to shut her mouth; her jaw had dropped a foot.

"Things have been so messed up with our family," Rusty's mom went on. "He's been awfully upset. I hope he hasn't been too much of a problem."

"No," Elsie stammered. "Not . . . much of a problem at all."

"Well, thank you," the woman said. "You're a miracle worker." The young woman walked away with her son in tow.

Elsie looked at me, her eyes wide. "Can I take that as a sign?" she finally whispered. "Do you think that's a sign from God?"

I was glad for the renewed hope on her face. We were both silent as we watched Rusty walk away with his mother.

"A little rough around the edges, maybe," I whispered, "but I think you might have a starfish."

Just then, the little boy turned around and stuck out his tongue at us.

I was surprised to hear Elsie laugh, this time a deep, happy laugh.

"Not quite a starfish," she said. "A minnow, perhaps. But, you know what? I'll take what I can get."

She laughed again, squared her shoulders, and walked back to her classroom.

BASKETS OF BLUEBELLS

The meadow was a sea of wildflowers flowing all the way to the hillside, where bluebells grew under every tree and bush, filling every shady space. Acres and acres of brilliant flowers, undulating with the early morning breeze. This would be the end of the bluebells, I knew, with summer just a heartbeat away. It was as if they were taking one last defiant stand before the heat came to claim them. I swallowed hard to get rid of the lump in my throat and stopped the school bus, pulling the bifold door open to get a better look.

The kids behind me were silent and motionless, all of them staring at the ocean of colors. I knew everyone, including me, was thinking about Evie.

Evie Stone had always seemed to be a truly beautiful person, both inside and out. When she walked with her thirteen-year-old daughter, Cori, to the bus stop each morning, I could barely tell them apart, both of them tall and thin with waist-length blond hair that danced in the breeze. Only the gray in Evie's hair and her smile that lit up the morning gave her away. Cori was the quiet one, pale and withdrawn, her own light dimmed by her mother's rainbow aura.

One of Evie's most charming habits was to meet the bus in the afternoon with a basket filled with wildflowers. She'd pick out a student, maybe someone who'd had trouble at school or at home with family, and fill their arms with the flowers, their hearts with laughter.

Baskets of Bluebells

"There's nothing in the world so bad that it can't be helped by a basket of bluebells," she told them, laughing.

How did she know a kid had a problem? I never did figure it out. Maybe she called the school or got the gossip from Cori. I preferred to think she just knew. That something inside her was tuned in to hurt and pain and reached out to help.

So great was her need to love and heal others that I couldn't believe or even pretend to understand what she did that Monday morning in October. Under a sky that was as brilliant blue as the bluebells, a morning so crisp you could smell autumn in the air, she waved goodbye to the bus, walked back to her car in the garage, got in, and started the engine. With the garage door tightly shut, she rested her head against the seat and closed her eyes.

That's where Cori found her that night, after the car had run out of gas, after Evie had run out of life.

What could have rested so heavily upon her soul that she finally decided she just couldn't face tomorrow? My stomach twisted into knots as I pictured her sweet smile, heard her voice.

But it was anger I felt, not sorrow. Fierce, unrelenting anger. I hated her for placing such a burden on her child's shoulders. Didn't she know it was the ones left behind who had to struggle with what she'd done? Had she even thought about the pain, the guilt that filled the hearts of those who loved her? I felt that Evie, who had always tried to ease the burdens of everyone she touched, had failed her own daughter.

"We were always kind of embarrassed to talk to each other," Cori told me not long after the funeral. "Now I tell her every day how much I love her. I tell her grave," she'd said, her voice cracking.

I watched her walk to the bus each morning, alone, smaller somehow, carrying an immeasurable burden upon her thin shoulders. And my anger burned hot and bright.

As bright as the bluebells this morning.

I sighed and dragged in a breath of the morning air, pungent with the scent of dew-wet wildflowers. It was time to go on. I reached for the door handle and started to shift the bus into drive when I felt a presence beside me.

"I need to go out for just a minute," the voice whispered. And Cori slipped past, down the steps, out into the sun-washed meadow. She knelt in the knee-deep flowers, picking the blooms, filling her arms.

Another high-schooler ran after her, then another. In a heartbeat, every kid on the bus was in the meadow picking the beautiful blooms. The quiet was shattered by giggles and laughter as the kids, all ages from kindergarten to high school, gathered armfuls of bluebells and dropped them into Cori's lap, over her head, heaping them until she almost disappeared. Even from where I sat, I could see the shaky smile on her lips, the hope in her eyes.

My radio crackled, and Mac's voice, obviously trying to be patient, said, "Number nine, do you think you might be on time this morning?"

Not this morning, I thought. "I'll be along in a bit," I told him. I smiled and turned the engine off so I could better hear the fun outside. In my opinion as the lowly bus driver, these kids needed these all too few minutes of bright sun along with a few grins and giggles.

In my heart, I heard Evie's words, "There's nothing in the world so bad that it can't be helped by a basket of bluebells."

I watched Cori laugh for the first time since her mom had died.

And I wanted to get my hands on Evie just one last time so I could shake her and make her see what she'd done. Force her to watch the children in the meadow gathering bluebells for her grieving daughter who shouldn't have to deal with anything more serious than wondering how short to cut her hair or what color dress to wear.

Oh, Evie, I thought, my anger fading at last to sorrow, *even though these flowers will wither in the heat of the approaching summer, in the coolness of spring they'll bloom again. That's how life is. But didn't you know? Death is forever.*

SOMEONE CARES

It's easy for a bus driver to form an opinion about what kind of an adult a particular child will grow into. And of course, as opinions go, a few don't pan out. The bright, promising kid will decide that disappearing into a drug-induced stupor is more interesting than making good grades in college; a troublemaker may happily surprise me and appear years later as pastor of a local church.

But I had been pretty sure I was right on target with Jason Germain. That's why I couldn't believe I was actually sitting there in the huge auditorium, listening to the tall, handsome man behind the podium. His hair was a little too long and shaggy—as usual—but still thick and dark. He was an impressive figure in the gray suit, radiating a confidence I'd never seen in his high-school days.

When I'd received the invitation, I thought it might be a joke, but here he was, Jason Germain, receiving the Man of the Year award from the city fathers. *Warden* Germain, head of the state prison. *How fitting*, I thought, since that's where I'd always suspected he'd end up. But I'd always thought if he wound up in the warden's office, it would be on the wrong side of the desk.

Jason had ridden my school bus from kindergarten on, and from the first, he was a trial. Not a truly mean kid, just overactive, loud, and outspoken. But it wasn't until high school that I began to fear for his future.

I remembered a particularly warm August morning. Jason had just gotten on the bus and walked to the back when I felt the bus rock curiously. I looked up in my overhead rearview mirror and saw him disappearing over the back of the seat on top of Chris Harker, a senior football player. I tore my seat belt loose and pushed my way to the back, but arms and fists were flying so fast, I was afraid to reach into the fray.

"Jason! Chris!" I yelled. The kids around them were screaming so loudly I knew no one could hear. Finally, I managed to get a hand on someone's shirt and pulled. Chris tumbled out of the seat and onto the floor. Before Jason could come after him, I shoved my body between them.

"That's all!" I panted. "You two are going to be spending time in the superintendent's office."

"He started it," Jason snarled. "He called me a . . ."

"No way!" Chris yelled back. "He grabbed my notebook and . . ."

The others were still jumping up and down in their seats, screaming and yelling as though they were at the circus. I thought briefly about leaving the bus parked alongside the road and hitchhiking back to town.

"Isn't there any way you guys can at least *try* to be civil to each other?" I asked.

"He's a jerk," Jason said.

"He needs a new brain," Chris responded.

Kids from the grade-schoolers all the way through the high-schoolers shouted opinions and smart remarks. Some were shoving others. And getting shoved back. The whole bus was out of control.

"Party's over," I yelled. "Sit down, please, or we're going to have the next party in the superintendent's office." I finally settled them all in their seats and got the whole show to the school. With great relief, I watched them all walk inside, someone else's problem for the day.

The animosity couldn't go on, but I didn't know what to do to change the atmosphere. Jason had set the standard, and it seemed as though every kid on the bus was going to follow suit. No one liked anyone else. No one wanted to merely get along. The crankiness and bickering went on and on. What a way to waste the entire school year.

Someone Cares

I didn't know what to do, and desperate people do desperate things. That night I typed a list of every kid on the bus and made forty-five copies, one for every rider. The next morning, I passed them out. The kids were silent for once, waiting for an explanation.

"OK," I said, "here's the deal. I want you to take these home and write out one thing you like about each person on this list. The ones who don't do it are going to be moved to the front seats."

The moans of disbelief and sarcasm were many and loud.

"Why do we have to do this?"

"There's nothing good about Scott."

"I hate Jason. What good can I say about him?"

All that week, they continued to complain, but with more threats and cajoling, gradually the lists began to come back in. When I had them all, I spent another night putting each name on a single sheet of paper, listing the things—anonymously—that each kid said about him or her. It took my whole evening. Would any of this even matter to these kids? I felt it was a waste of time, but the next morning, when I handed out the new sheets, there was silence on the bus. I kept looking back in the rearview mirror, astonished that there was no commotion as they read. I saw some of them occasionally glance around the bus. It was difficult to read the expressions. What did they think? Was this a mistake?

It didn't take long for things to get back to normal. The teasing and arguing went on, but at least there were no more brawls. The lists were never mentioned again. It was as I expected. I chalked it up to a life experience and went on, glad I didn't have to break up a fist fight every day, convinced there's very little a school-bus driver can do to change the world.

Today, years later, I was delighted to be attending the awards ceremony, glad to see that at least one of the kids I'd taken to school had his life on track—no matter what I'd secretly thought years ago. It was a pleasant and welcome surprise.

"Mrs. Gulley?" A young woman stopped by my seat. I had no idea who she was. "Sheila," she said, laughing. "I'm Sheila Casten . . . all grown up."

She stepped aside, and I had no doubt who the young man was.

"Hi, Chris," I said. Chris Harker's face and shoulders hadn't lost the solid, muscular look of a football player.

"I'm *Mrs*. Harker, now," Sheila said.

"That's wonderful," I said. And meant it. "I'm so glad to see all of you today. What a super occasion for us all to get together."

As we were talking, I saw Jason walking toward us. He stopped and smiled. I was struck again by the maturity, the confidence on his face, in his eyes, so unlike the angry child on my bus years ago.

"Hi, Warden Germain," I said. "Been in any good fights lately?"

They all laughed. Then Jason reached for his pocket. He pulled a bit of paper from his wallet, yellowed with age.

"I'm so glad you came today," he said. "I've always wanted to show you this." He unfolded it. I saw what it was and looked up at him, stunned.

"It's the list I gave you," I said.

Jason nodded. "I've kept this since that day on the bus," he said. "You can't imagine how surprised I was to know that some of the kids actually saw good in me. I never knew I meant anything to anyone."

"Hey," Chris said, pulling out his own wallet. He unfolded a similar sheet of paper.

Sheila's cheeks reddened. "I put mine in our wedding album," she said. "My friend Jan saved hers in her diary. I'll bet we all saved them."

My eyes blurred with tears.

"All those years," I told them, "I never thought anything I did mattered to the kids on my bus."

Jason's smile was big, and his voice was soft. "It mattered to us," he said. "Thank you for showing us someone cared."

JUST ANOTHER SUMMER

It was the last day of school before summer vacation. For weeks, I'd been driving my school bus down roads that were narrow ribbons of slush, muddy water sloshing across the windshield as the front wheels boomed through bottomless holes and ruts.

Now summer had taken care of the nasty parts of spring and was busy intensifying the good. Normally, I loved the brilliant green of the spring wheat, the new blueness of the sky, the bright crocuses that barely raised their heads through the still-cool earth.

Somehow, none of it mattered today.

I felt none of the giddy sense of renewal, the lightness in my heart that came with the knowledge of a long, lazy summer stretching in front of me. For me, this summer was bringing painful decisions, transitions that would change my life forever, heartache mixed with a tremendous pride and happiness.

This was the year I graduated from high school for the final time. Soon, my youngest son, Jeff, would leave to begin a life of his own, and I would no longer have a vested interest in our small school system.

Jeff and his classmates were wide-eyed kindergartners at the time I became an equally wide-eyed fledgling driver. I had hauled many of them to school for thirteen years, watched as they grew from babies into young adults, suffered through their problems, and rejoiced in their happiness.

Three of them were now just tragic memories; others had been disappointed by what life had handed them and become cold and distrustful. But most were reaching forward with hearts full of hope, anxious for whatever was to come, the look in their eyes still reminiscent of that beautiful innocence I had seen the first day they climbed up the steps into the bus. *They're ready to move on, and I'll be left behind,* I thought.

The circle had been completed. I wasn't sure that I wanted to continue to pull up to the high school every day, knowing that there was no one inside who belonged to me. I wasn't sure that I could continue to struggle with the intensity of the responsibilities, the emotional rollercoaster of holding sixty lives in my hands for two hours every day.

Maybe I really didn't want to drive a school bus all the rest of my life.

A shout from the back of the bus brought me out of my thoughts with a jolt.

"Mrs. Gulley! Look!"

Wildly looking about for whatever calamity had befallen, I finally saw the three furry red shapes scrambling down the side of the road. A mama fox and her two kits. I braked to a stop, and we watched, murmurs of delight coming from even the coolest of the high-schoolers in the back.

There was a presence at my elbow. Vicki, a tall, lanky sixth-grader unconsciously put her hand on my arm as she watched the fox family disappear into a culvert. She looked at me, her eyes bright with excitement. "Did you see?" she whispered. "Did you see?"

I nodded, laughing, sharing her thrill. I searched her face as she chattered on, not really hearing her words. I was looking for the shy baby I'd picked up one fall morning seven years before. *Almost gone,* I thought. A woman-child moving in to take her place, showing a hint of the beauty she was to become. I saw her glance into the overhead mirror and self-consciously touch her freshly permed hair. Last year she didn't even bother to carry a comb.

My gaze and my thoughts wandered back to little Doug, asleep in the corner of his seat after a tough day in first grade. Before he got off the bus, I wanted to tell him all about the fox and her children. I knew him well enough to know how excited he'd be. The world still held wonder for him.

In the middle-school seats, Cathy stared out the window, but her eyes were dark and empty. Her parents had divorced just after Christmas, and Cathy had retreated into a quiet little world all her own, where she was safe from the brutal realities of life. I worried about her.

Near the back of the bus, I caught a glimpse of Adam, who had already lost interest in the foxes and was back to his usual pastime of teasing every girl within reach. A freshman, low man on the totem pole this year. I knew his teasing covered up a lot of insecurity. Sometimes on a quiet morning, I could look back in my overhead mirror and, just for an instant, catch the scared little boy peeking out from the handsome man's face.

Wonders, all of them. Like the spring gone by and the approaching summer. Like the family of red foxes who had flashed in front of us. My eyes swept across their faces. What would they be in years to come? How would their lives flow?

It was getting late. I asked Vicki to get back to her seat, and we moved on down the road to her driveway. I opened the door to let her out, and somehow the air smelled sweeter, fresher. I took a deep breath, and my heart felt lighter.

Vicki paused at the door.

"Have a nice summer, Mrs. Gulley," she said. "See you next year."

I watched her walk up the driveway. I couldn't stop the smile that spread across my face.

Yes, Vicki, I thought, *I think you will.*

IF YOU ENJOYED THIS BOOK, YOU'LL ENJOY THESE AS WELL:

Even the Angels Must Laugh—Again

Jan Doward. This hilarious book is back in print! Jan Doward has added more stories that will really crack you up! Baptisms that boggle the mind, church bloopers that almost bring down the house, evangelism beyond belief—each chapter is filled with the joy of worshiping with human beings. Story by story, this collection of humor will remind you of the joy of being a Christian and the wonder of a God who created laughter.

0-8163-1408-X. Paperback.

US$5.99, Can$8.99.

Lighthearted Devotions

Author *Wayne Taylor* blends a hearty dash of humor with a generous dose of wisdom, to bring you this delightfully delicious collection of real-life parables about childhood mischief, academy pranks, college stunts, and army adventures.

0-8163-1784-4. Paperback.

US$6.99, Can$10.49.

Owney the Post Office Dog and Other Great Dog Stories

Joe L. Wheeler. Known for collecting stories that require keeping tissues handy, Joe L. Wheeler introduces a new anthology of nostalgic dog tales that will thrill, inspire, and cause you to feel young no matter your age. Beautifully written and suitable for the whole family, this book celebrates the timeless virtues of loyalty, honor, friendship, and devotion through tales that are among the most moving and memorable you'll ever read.

0-8163-2045-4. Paperback.

US$12.99, Can$19.49.

Order from your ABC by calling **1-800-765-6955**, or get online and shop our virtual store at **www.adventistbookcenter.com**.

- Read a chapter from your favorite book
- Order online
- Sign up for email notices on new products

Prices subject to change without notice.